I AM JENNIFER

I AM JENNIFER

Not the Boy I Thought I Was Supposed to Be

JENNIFER GROSS

 iUniverse®

I AM JENNIFER
NOT THE BOY I THOUGHT I WAS SUPPOSED TO BE

KJV
Scripture quotations marked KJV are from the Holy Bible, King James Version (Authorized Version). First published in 1611. Quoted from the KJV Classic Reference Bible, Copyright © 1983 by The Zondervan Corporation.

iUniverse books may be ordered through booksellers or by contacting:

iUniverse
1663 Liberty Drive
Bloomington, IN 47403
www.iuniverse.com
1-800-Authors (1-800-288-4677)

ISBN: 978-1-5320-8362-4 (sc)
ISBN: 978-1-5320-8363-1 (e)

Library of Congress Control Number: 2019914719

Print information available on the last page.

iUniverse rev. date: 09/21/2019

To parents everywhere

ACKNOWLEDGEMENTS

Many thanks to my friend Shirley, who gave me the title of the book: *I Am Jennifer*. Thanks to my friendly editor, David Boyce, who encouraged me to narrow my focus to what was most important. Thank you Kate D., editor from iUniverse, for your proficiency in editing. Your comments were exceptionally helpful. Also, many thanks to my family and friends for your support and advice, especially you Mom.

INTRODUCTION

Ever felt it? Not the sudden flash of explosive, passionate anger but the slow, consuming ember in the pit of your stomach. I have. I am not sure why it's there, not sure how it began, but absolutely sure it cannot be quenched by the trivial attempts of those who are aware enough to sense it. I'm not sure who I am.

Anger, frustration, and sadness finally consumed me to the point of no return. I had to know. I would do anything to know.

Gripped with an overwhelming sense of despair, I climbed on my bed. In my mind, I screamed at God, "Why? Why am I such a negative person towards myself and others? Why can't I love *me*? Why do I feel I have to live in hell and don't deserve to be happy in this life? Why, God? Why?" The year was 1986.

It is now 2019. How did I get here? Let me go back to the beginning and lay the foundation for this remarkable journey of self-discovery.

I was born Miriam in the early 1950s in Canada. Dad wanted boys, a whole slew of them, to staff his baseball and football teams. Mom thought I was going to be an athlete because I was more active in her womb than her two previous daughters. Back in the 1950s, who were athletes? Boys.

CHAPTER 1

THE FARM

Even though I was born in Winnipeg, Manitoba, my grandparents' farm is where I spent my childhood and where my memories of my dad began. I was 4 years old when our family moved to my dad's parents' farm in eastern Manitoba.

Oh my … the farm. The farm buildings were situated in the heart of 320 flat, boggy, heavily treed acres, or a half section of land—a section being one square mile. Most of the buildings were snuggled up to the fifty-five-feet-wide river that meandered through the land. The main gravel road was a mile away. Half of our lane followed the landscape carved out by the river. Grandpa had cleared about half the land, and in 1929, he built the house, barn, and implement sheds.

The farm was very isolated. One of our closest neighbours was my dad's brother and his family, who lived two miles away. One of their daughters became my closest friend and still is to this day.

A Hutterite colony was about a quarter of a mile on the other side of the main gravel road. Hutterites are German-speaking religious refugees who came to North America in the 1870s under the guidance of Jakob Hutter. They live in colonies and are similar to the Mennonites and the Amish, who are also farmers. Some colonies specialize in cattle, some in pigs, and some in fowl.

Besides the two-room schoolhouse in the Hutterite colony, which accommodated grades 1 through 3, there were two one-room schoolhouses within a ten-mile radius of the farm. In these schools, one teacher taught all eight elementary grades. The closest town, Beausejour, was nineteen miles away and where the regional high school was located and also where my family went to church. Winnipeg, the Big Town, was thirty miles west of the farm.

The seasons were delightful. Colours burst as flowers bloomed and butterflies arrived in spring, the air heavily scented with lilacs and freshly cut grass. Summer brought hot, muggy days when sweat broke out just from moving a finger. With autumn came smells of wet earth mingled with newly fallen leaves. Winter arrived with crisp, cold, moonlit nights, and the crunch of footsteps on snow could be heard from what seemed like miles away.

During all of the seasons, the stillness of the air amplified the sounds of cattle lowing, horses neighing, dogs barking, cats meowing, pigs contemplating their next realm of existence, geese honking, and chickens clucking. All were the wonderful and satisfying sights, sounds, and smells of the farm.

We grew feed for the animals, and they fed us (except for the cats and dogs!). Because our farm was one of the first to have electricity, we were quite self-sufficient. Most produce from the garden was processed for the winter months, as were the wild berries (chokecherries, pin cherries, saskatoons, blueberries) and plums found on the land. Grandpa kept bees, so we had freshly extracted honey. Yum.

A national forest reserve butted up against the farm. We had many adventures with deer, cranes, snapping turtles, skunks, and many other native animals. Beavers dammed the river. A snowy owl missed me by inches as I stood in our driveway. A bear—probably a black bear—came within two hundred feet of the house before heading for the river. Yapping coyotes could be heard almost every one of the long summer nights.

When we moved to the farm, I was extraordinarily shy. I was 4 but hadn't spoken yet. Thank goodness Grandpa introduced me to those wonderful *animals*. Animals didn't care if I remained silent, cried a lot, or kept to myself. They showed me true, unconditional acceptance. I started speaking. They listened. *We are here for you*, I heard them say in my mind.

CHAPTER 2

DAD

Dad and I got along quite well to begin with. He was short, only five feet, eight inches tall, but powerfully built like his dad, who could carry one-hundred-pound bags of feed under each arm. He had a ruddy complexion and loved being physically active, baseball being a favourite activity. He even played semipro ball as a catcher with a reputation for "soft hands".

Unfortunately, "explosive anger" and "Dad" seemed synonymous. We children were to be seen and not heard. No discussion included children. In fact, I was terrified of asking for or saying anything for fear it would upset him. If Dad didn't like what he saw or heard—ouch, that strap stung. It was actually called a *strop*: a flexible strap for sharpening razors. It was about eighteen inches long, two inches wide, and almost an inch thick. Dad would spank us in anger and almost always on a bare bottom.

Two incidents stick out in my mind. My brother had just been strapped for something. As Dad finished and was turning to leave, my brother stuck his tongue out at him. His face contorting with anger, Dad reached for my brother again.

The other time, I was about 9 years old and was caught innocently kissing a cousin. "Miriam, I'll teach you never to kiss a boy," Dad said as he laid it on thick and heavy.

He also couldn't stand noise. One night he shot a dog that wouldn't stop barking. I later learned that the dog had had a mean disposition.

Since I rarely spoke, I didn't get strapped as often as my siblings. I was the peacemaker; there was no ruffling of feathers when the feathers felt like whips. Yet in spite of all the negativity, I loved being Dad's helper.

Occasionally his fun side would surface. Crouching down on all fours, he'd let us kids climb onto his back and be taken for piggyback rides. We played with the air sacs of the fish he caught, and he'd make balloons out of them. He took part in organizing school parades and sports days. During the summer, we'd stop for ice-cream on Sunday afternoons on the way home from church. I became Daddy's little helper. I helped weed the enormous garden, took lunches out to the working men in the haying fields, prepared the chop to feed to the cows while Dad milked them, and many other chores. I was quite a helpful child.

I loved being a tomboy, not only by physically helping out on the farm but also by playing sports. Exhilaration abounded when I sailed over the high jump. In baseball, I was thrilled every time I threw someone out at home base. I had a very accurate throwing arm and often played outfielder during recess. I eschewed anything to do with chores within the home.

CHAPTER 3

MOM

Mom was as tall as Dad and wouldn't wear high heels, as that would make her taller. She was a stay-at-home mother, not least because she had her first five children in seven years. She was kind of busy! She also had decided, long before she ever met Dad, that she was *not* going to let others raise *her* children.

I don't have many memories of her. She always seemed to be in the background. She was quiet, in direct contrast to Dad. She had grown up in a household where her mom yelled most of the time; therefore Mom vowed never to behave in that way. She played her role as dutiful housewife very well, rarely talking back to Dad. She supported him through everything, especially living on the farm, even though she had never lived on one before. Her faith in God and family life never wavered.

She was the buffer between Dad and us. She let us explore and get into almost anything, within reason. Even though she was terrified of the river, she would sit on the bank and watch us having a blast, never once giving us the impression that she was extremely anxious. She was very patient as she watched us prolong our dishwashing duties— none of us, it seemed, liked to do the dishes. We would complain for what seemed like hours, but we *always* ended up doing them.

CHAPTER 4

A BROTHER

When I was 5 years old, along came my brother. Exactly one week separated our birthdays. Wow! And here was someone I could eventually play with and just hang out with.

I eagerly got the cloth diapers to help change him, and I anxiously awaited the time when he could join me in playing hockey and roughhousing.

Later on, as he grew, confusion crept into my mind. I asked him, "Why are you treated differently? Why won't Dad and Mom let you sleep with us girls in the attic? Why do you sleep on the couch instead?" He had no answer.

Playing hockey with him on the frozen winter road, with bales of straw for goalposts, was one of my favourite winter pastimes.

Wood for the furnace was stored in the basement. One fall, the task of getting it into the basement fell on me and my brother. The quickest way was to open a basement window and chuck it in. My brother passed the wood to me, and I chucked it. Perhaps because he was getting tired, one time he missed my hands and ploughed me in the head instead, cutting open a gash. Mom just put something on it to stop the bleeding, and out I went again to continue the chore.

CHAPTER 5

CHURCH

Religion ruled our lives. Grandpa was Catholic and Grandma was Lutheran. We were members of The Church of Jesus Christ of Latter-day Saints. Not only was Dad a strict disciplinarian of Austrian and Hungarian ancestry, but he was so enthusiastic about his religion that most people today would call him a fanatic. Practically everything he said was quoted from Scripture.

Paraphrasing John 15:19 KJV, he told us we were to "be in the world but not of the world." Therefore, we had no influence in the home other than what came through the church. Dad's life seemed to consist of trying to be perfect in daily Scripture, meal and family prayers, and church attendance, regardless of inclement weather or sickness. His admonition was "never turn down a church calling", as it was a lay ministry. He took to heart the words of David O. McKay, a Latter-day prophet who taught that success in the home is

13

the most important success one can achieve in this lifetime.Yet Dad never seemed to be home. Quite often he was out helping someone else or attending church meetings. His love of the church shone through as he served with all his heart, even naming three of us children after biblical characters.

He must have felt great pressure to live the commandments so perfectly. Perhaps his anger was his disappointment when he failed to live up to those standards. I felt the same way. Perfection was the key to a good life.

Because the church reinforced the social norm that the man was head of the house, Dad's word was law. Usually it was the *only* law. Councils were held to inform, not to debate and decide. Dad's was the *only* way, with no tolerance for differing points of view. He loved the letter of the law but seemed to have a problem with the spirit of it.

The church, in addition to the culture of the fifties, taught that the only goals for women were to marry, have children, and raise them in righteousness. If the opportunity didn't present itself in this life, it would in the next. Men were to be breadwinners, decision-makers, lawmakers, and discipliners. Women were to be mothers and caregivers in the home. My mom and dad vigorously promoted these teachings.

The Church of Jesus Christ of Latter-day Saints has a lay ministry. All appointments, positions, and callings within the church are supposed to be done by the Spirit of the Holy Ghost, which is bestowed on newly baptized members. Therefore, anyone who is deemed worthy can become a bishop, a counsellor, or president of church programs such as the Sunday school, the primary (classes for children ages three to twelve), the young women's or young men's associations, and the Relief Society, which is the women's organization.

The men advance through stages of the holy priesthood—first the Aaronic priesthood and then the Melchizedek priesthood—which allows them to be considered for the position of president of the church itself.

Because the church was so small in our area, it was called a "branch", not a "ward". Many people wore many hats. I was taught to never say no to any church authority. I took it to heart that this meant I was to agree to do whatever I was asked. Since only men were allowed to hold the priesthood, in my mind, that meant I was to obey every man. The only men I knew who weren't members of the church were my grandpa and the milkman who came weekly to buy milk, eggs, and cream. Every other man held a position of authority in the church, and I was never, ever to say no.

CHAPTER 6

MUSIC

Since Grandpa and Grandma had the only TV in our household, we were left with the radio and gramophone. Opera and musicals from the 1930s to 1950s were allowed, as Mom loved her musicals, especially Nelson Eddy and Jeannette McDonald. Bing Crosby and Dean Martin were also acceptable, but no Frank Sinatra—probably because he was on a communist-sympathizers list—and *definitely* no rock and roll. *That* was of the Devil. Therefore we never listened to Elvis Presley, the Beatles, or anyone who sounded and acted like them.

Mom had a lovely alto voice and Dad a wonderful tenor. Dad seemed happiest when singing or performing, as he was a bit of a ham. We sang mostly in church.

Dad was very proud of us children when we accomplished anything musically, and he loved to show us off to visitors. My two older sisters played the piano while the rest of us sang. He often spoke of putting together a band. At church dances, he delighted in his favourite dances, which included the polka, schottische, and waltz. Dad also whistled. "I Am a Happy Wanderer" was a favourite of his. To this day, I love to hear someone whistling.

Whenever Mom and Dad were both away at church meetings, especially in winter, we would break out the gramophone, dress up, and dance to the old 78 rpm records. What a great time we had. One night we must have been overly enthusiastic, as a knock came on the adjoining wall. The next day, Grandma told Mom that she had banged on the wall because of the noise, and had been quite surprised when we actually quit making the noise! Did I mention that my grandparents lived right next door in the same house? Yes, Grandpa and Grandma's house was like a duplex, with a doorway between the two sides. One side was their summer home, which included a large dining room/kitchen, one bedroom, and no basement, but had a large porch for storing stuff. The other side contained a kitchen, living room, two small bedrooms, an attic accessed by stairs, and a basement containing a wood-burning furnace and cold food storage. Our family lived in this side, while Grandpa and Grandma had the summer side.

CHAPTER 7

SEX AND LOVE

Puberty!

I was 11 years old. One bright, sunny day in late spring, while I was at school, I noticed blood on my panties. I came home and asked, "Why am I bleeding?" Mom explained the menstrual cycle to me. It didn't make any sense: something about blood flowing and eggs, and it was going to go on for a long, long time.

A few months later, I was asking, "What's happening to me and what are these bumps on my chest?" *Maybe I can burn them off*, I thought as I stood before a roaring furnace with a lit match in hand.

Well, that didn't work. The emotional scars lasted much longer than the physical ones.

Sex, lust, and fornication were all forbidden subjects. "Neither shalt thou desire thy neighbour's wife" (Deut. 5:21 KJV). I knew very well what lurked in the mind of every man. Sex was very frowned upon for the unmarried. It seemed that the only reason for sex was to procreate. Mom and Dad rarely showed affection other than a goodbye peck on the cheek.

Modesty was very important in our home. "Clothe yourselves properly" was a constant refrain. Nothing sleeveless was allowed, even in the summer heat, and certainly no tight clothing. Little if any make-up was worn.

Kissing seemed to be on the same level as the other sins. Dad spanked me for it, saying, "I'll teach you to never kiss a boy." Sex education consisted of railing against these sins. We weren't even allowed to watch the mating of two horses. "Stay in the house," we were told in no uncertain terms.

What was love, really?

CHAPTER 8

MORE FARM MEMORIES

At age 6, I started school at the Hutterite colony. Terrified of meeting new people, I cried all day.

As time went on, I became more aware of the outside world. Because Dad taught in many of the one-room country schools to supplement his income, we changed schools often, getting to know more people.

When I was 10 or 11, I attended the same school where Dad taught. What an eye-opener that was. The school had a rougher group of kids than I'd ever seen. "Teacher's pet" rang in my ears constantly because of my good grades. The other kids didn't believe it was because I had to do my homework every day and was constantly being corrected at home: "may" versus "can", "good" versus "well", "police" not "cops", and so forth. Not much confidence-building happened at that school.

Jennifer Gross

We four sisters were all horse crazy. Grandma overcame her fear of us getting hurt and allowed us to ride the old workhorses. Barney was a percheron cross and Daisy a shire cross. We would take the buggy out to get the mail. Daisy pulled the buggy and Barney was ridden as the outrider. I wanted to be a trick rider, so I practised on Barney without a saddle, standing on his huge rump and galloping around the yard. When he learned voice commands, he was much more manageable.

A neighbour found out about how horse crazy we were and gave us a standing invitation to ride his horses whenever we wanted to. "Just let the caretaker know you're coming." The neighbour lived in Winnipeg, the Big City, and the horses were stabled at his family's weekend retreat. These horses were *real* riding horses. The dad's horse was a registered Quarter Horse, and the mom rode a palomino which had toured Canada and the United States as a jumper. The palomino's trot was smooth as silk and her gallop was like a rocking chair, no saddle needed. Their older child rode a Welsh pony, the one I usually rode. The younger child rode a Shetland pony, which trotted when everyone else was galloping! Thus there were four horses for four girls: heaven.

Chores were plentiful. We teamed up to do dishes. We hauled water from the well—which was, of course, at the *bottom* of the hill. We brought the cows in from the pasture, which was located across the river, with the help of our Scotch collie, Lassie. We mowed the lawn with a push mower and weeded an enormous garden. It took all day to do the wash with the wringer washing machine and clothes line. We helped with the fall harvest of wheat, oats, and alfalfa.

I remember watching Dad milk the cows in the early hours of a summer day. We girls played house, laying out walls with raked leaves and snitching veggies from the garden for tea. I saw a litter of kittens being born. I watched my oldest sister teach our old dogs new tricks (jumping over sticks), teach old horses new tricks (obey voice commands), and teach a three-month-old calf to accept a halter, saddle, and rider!

I marvelled at Grandma's skill with a wood stove. I gathered eggs and watched chicks grow big, only to be killed in the fall. I plucked their dead, stinky feathers to prepare them for the freezer. I saw horses pulling hay wagons around the fields and taking out the stoneboat (a large, flat piece of iron bolted to runners) piled high with manure to spread.

We had no indoor plumbing, though there was a large cistern in the basement that collected rainwater to be used in winter. We had an outhouse. I was terrified of using it after dark, as the yard light didn't extend all the way to the other side of the tractor garage. There was a huge caragana hedge right in front of it. The bogeyman was sure to get me! Real toilet paper was a luxury that didn't happen often. Eaton's catalogues were very useful.

I remember dancing in the warm summer rain in our swimsuits. We found a snapping turtle on the road and a black widow spider down by the river. I listened to one of my sisters make up stories about a boy named Junior who had many wonderful adventures—always recounted when we were supposed to be asleep. Often, too, I read under the covers with a flashlight.

Occasionally, our cousins from Winnipeg spent the summer months with us. We dared one to eat a live minnow—and he did! I loved to chase the sissy town boys with large but harmless garter snakes. Prisoner's base was a favourite game, as were cowboys and Indians and cops and robbers. The horses were used as the getaway vehicles in the latter two activities.

Grandpa grew specialized seed that was then sold back to the farmers. Therefore, his crops had to pass inspection: not one mustard plant was allowed to grow to fruition in the fields. One year Dad asked us to go into the wheat fields and pick all the noxious mustard plants we could see. They were the only plants with yellow flowers. He promised us a penny for every two we picked. Off we four girls went, sporting sunbonnets as we walked through grain that was almost as tall as we were. I think Dad shelled out a total of about $1.50. After about a week, we thought we'd found them all, but the grain inspector found the single one we'd missed. Grandpa had to talk long and hard to convince him it was the *only* one. Unless the inspector believed him, Grandpa wouldn't get paid.

Yes, the inspector believed him.

Winter activities included watching the Montreal Canadiens on *Hockey Night in Canada* every Saturday night, taking baths in a big metal tub in the kitchen, and pulling cars out of the ditch that ran beside our mile-long lane. Many times Dad had to leave our car at the mailbox out on the main road.

Getting a Christmas tree from the bush across the river was always fun. One year a few of us got into the huge toboggan-style sled (long, with high sides). With the horse pulling and Dad at the back, we set off. The horse loved to run. Around a corner we went at a full gallop, tipped over, and spilled out, laughing as we did so. We did eventually get our tree.

Our family took Grandma to her traditional church Christmas concerts just down the road, where Santa would show up. We'd each get a little paper bag that had one orange, a few hard candies, and some nuts in it.

One of my best memories was when the horses were hitched to the grain wagon that was on runners for the winter. We all piled onto hay bales and wrapped ourselves in toasty-warm Hudson Bay blankets. With harness bells ringing and Christmas carols escaping our cold lips, we clip-clopped to our cousin's place two miles down the road for a Christmas celebration.

On the farm, I was safe—safe from strangers, safe from the evils of the world. I was hidden. My farm life was my refuge.

 CHAPTER 9

CULTURE SHOCK

I had lived on the farm for eight and a half mostly happy years when, in September 1965, at the age of 13, I abruptly moved with my family to Utah in the United States. Culture shock! I went from a one-room, twenty-student school to a two-storey, four-hundred-student school. I was in eighth grade. *Gulp.* At church there were two to three hundred people instead of thirty-five or forty.

Even the house we lived in seemed big and luxurious. It even had running water! My mom's dad had passed away the previous year, so we moved in with Grandma, as she was very lonely. She had the main level of the house while we took possession of the upstairs.

Though we were definitely hicks from the back country, we had impeccable manners. Because Americans didn't know much about Canada, they believed *anything* we said. We convinced them that Canadians lived in igloos, drove dog sleds, and didn't have refrigerators. That part was fun.

But the rest was terrible, at least for me. The phrase "Oh, how *gross*" became popular. As our last name was Gross, I started to hate my name. Because we were from Canada, everyone assumed we spoke French. It was true that our Canadian teachers had been obligated to teach us French, but unfortunately my teachers hadn't known it well enough to speak it, just to write it. I was laughed at when I couldn't speak it in French class, though I did show off when I received As for writing it. To make my life easier, I often hid in the school library. I made only one friend all year.

Church headquarters were located in Salt Lake City, Utah. It was very different to have many church members right next door to us. In fact, there were about three hundred of us in roughly a six-block area. I was confused though. It seemed these members weren't interested in living the commandments the way I had been taught to do. They seemed much more relaxed, not so intently focused on being perfect. They also seemed to think the church was the be-all and end-all of everything religious, whereas I had been taught that a testimony of Christ's divinity was most important.

Dad had a hard time finding work in Salt Lake City. Even though he had twenty years of teaching experience and a teacher's certificate, he didn't have a degree. He went back to Canada to try his luck there. He found a teaching job at a Hutterite colony near Brandon, Manitoba, about three hours west of Winnipeg. We crossed the US/Canadian border on 1 January 1967, belting out "O Canada" at the top of our lungs. It happened to be Canada's centennial year.

Six of us lived in the tiny two-bedroom teacherage on the colony. Mom and Dad had one bedroom, three of us girls had the other, and my brother slept on the living room couch. I was the oldest at home, at age 14, and the other kids were 13, 9, and 2.

Because grade 9 was not taught at the colony, I took it by correspondence, which gave me time to look after my youngest sister. At least, she was the youngest at that time. Once again Dad displayed his attitude toward noise. My 2-year-old sister seemed to cry all the time, perhaps because Mom was helping Dad teach and therefore was not at home as much as usual.

My sister had nightmares, and many times I held her on our bed, rocking, rocking, rocking to soothe her. It usually worked. One night, though, it didn't. Dad came into the room, yanked her from my arms, and put her outdoors. Shutting the door, he said, "I'll teach you to behave." It was winter, and she was wearing nothing but her nightgown. He left her there for only a few minutes, but I was fuming, albeit only within myself. Perhaps this was the start of my growing dislike for him, and also for my feeling of helplessness to stand up to him.

That summer, we went to the farm for a visit. Since most of my memories there were happy ones, I persuaded Mom and Dad to let me stay for most of the summer.

On a particularly beautiful, sunny day, I decided to go riding. I set out eagerly, anticipating a great ride. As Honey's powerful Quarter Horse body surged beneath me, the wind whipped through my hair and her mane. It was glorious freedom.

Then the milkman showed up.

CHAPTER 10

LESSONS LEARNED

He was the same milkman who had bought eggs, milk, and cream from my grandparents when I lived on the farm. He apparently still had the job. On this day, when he saw me riding, he slowed down the truck and called me over. He offered me an ice cream, which had been a favourite treat in years gone by. At this time, I was 15 years old, still extremely shy and naive.

He approached me while I was sitting on the horse and put his hand on my leg above the knee, smiling and talking as he did so. I immediately felt uncomfortable, uneasy. Finally he removed it. *I must not let him catch me alone again*, I thought.

It didn't work. A few days later, I was walking along the main road after getting the mail, and I saw his truck coming. I went into the field, hoping he would keep going, but he didn't. He called me over to get an ice cream. When I finished it, he put me on his lap, fondling my rear as he did so.

Once I was seated on his lap, he fondled my breasts and inner thighs. I was almost in tears. "*Never say no*" rang in my head. He finally stopped and drove off.

I walked down the road towards the farm, crying until I could barely see through the stream of tears. My day was ruined—and not just a single day. My thoughts ran in circles. *Why did I let this happen? How could I let it happen? I'm a terrible person. I must have made myself attractive to him. Oh no! Dad is going to kill me if he ever finds out. What am I going to do?*

That night, as I touched the places the milkman had touched, searing pain shot through my body, bringing me to tears once again. I felt guilt, shame, and despair.

I couldn't go to Dad. Since Mom stood behind Dad in every decision, I couldn't go to her either. I confided in no one. I was alone—and lonely.

Later that summer, I was told I would be spending my high school years with my grandma in the US. I was being sent away, abandoned!

Spiralling inward, I found solace only in thinking of ways to escape. I couldn't go to anyone outside of the family. That was strictly forbidden, and I didn't purposely do forbidden things. My only recourse seemed to be suicide. Almost every waking moment of my first year in high school was focused on how I could do it. I cried almost every night because I didn't have the guts to go ahead with the plan, whether it was pills, slashing my wrists, or walking in front of a bus.

The second year was better. I made two friends.

The third year was the best. A teacher befriended me. I thought, *Perhaps life is worth living.*

Following high school, I returned to Canada and became active in church: teaching children, filling secretarial positions in its different organizations, organizing the library, and even serving a one-and-a-half-year mission, though at first I was determined not to do so.

There are many different kinds of missions one could serve in The Church of Jesus Christ of Latter-day Saints: proselytizing, humanitarian, construction, medical, and so forth. Usually men were 18 to 21 years old and were addressed as Elder so and so, using last names only, and women were 19 and older and were addressed as Sister so and so. Retired single men and women, along with couples were also sent to one of many places in the world to proselytize. Men were paired with men and women with women except for the couples of course. They went two by two and usually door to door, teaching about Christ according to the Bible and the Book of Mormon, a book of scripture about Christ's visit to the Americas shortly before his ascension to heaven.

One of my sisters returned home from her mission. She had been the first in our family to go on one. A few weeks before she was due back, my church friends and family began questioning me: "Miriam, when are you going?"

"I don't know."

"Miriam, where would you like to go?"

"I don't know."

"Miriam, have you sent your papers in yet?"

"No."

"Miriam, have you spoken with the bishop yet?"

"No."

I was bound and determined *not* to go, yet when the bishop called me in to discuss the possibility, I knew I could give only one answer: "Yes." One didn't say no to a church calling. After all, if you were called, it was because that call was divinely inspired.

It was culture shock all over again. I was plopped down in Florida with little preparation for what a mission entailed. It was a highly organized, intense time. I rose at six o'clock in the morning for prayers, Scripture study, and breakfast. I was out the door by nine to walk the streets of whatever town I was in, looking for those who might be interested in hearing what I had to say. Then I went home for lunch and was back out on the streets for the afternoon. After supper, I hoped to have an actual appointment each day to teach someone about gospel principles. All this was done with a companion who was attached at my hip, or so it seemed. We were *never* to be out of each other's sight or earshot.

Despite the shock of it, man, did I love being around all those elders. Wow! At district meetings, when three or four sets of missionaries met for instruction, I related much more to them than to the sisters. They were more interesting to be around. If one of them had any kind of good singing voice, I would hang around him as much as possible—a plus when looking for a potential husband. Zone conferences were the best. Forty or fifty of us would gather to receive instructions directly from our mission president. There were only four or five other pairs of women missionaries in my whole mission, the Florida South Mission, which ranged from south of Ocala to the northern tip of South America, and also included Puerto Rico.

I learned that Heavenly Father and Jesus were real. I was challenged by a Church of Christ minister to find out if what I was teaching was truth. I was on my knees one night when I poured out my soul to Heavenly Father. I truly wanted to know. Eventually an extraordinarily powerful feeling ran down from my head to my toes, filling my spirit with a warm, comforting feeling and an instant knowledge that Heavenly Father and Jesus were real and loved me. Teaching with that spirit became an absolute delight as I saw people accept that spirit into their lives.

After I came home from my mission, I thought I would be happy for the rest of my life. Not quite. I couldn't find a job, and I wasn't accepted at university. My plans were going down the drain. Within a year, my happy feelings had faded away. I came to realize I was the same unhappy person I'd always been. Why? What had happened? Didn't having a testimony of Heavenly Father and Jesus mean that I was perfect? That I wouldn't have any more problems in life? Didn't I deserve everything that was good?

CHAPTER 11

INTROSPECTION

As I wrestled with these questions, for the first time I analysed myself. These were my conclusions:

- I hated being a girl.
- I enjoyed physical activity.
- My brother and I were close.
- Boy stuff was great, fun, and exciting.
- Girls were a bore, as all they ever talked about were clothes, boyfriends (yuck), sewing, and homemaking.

I was 25 years old.

As I looked back on my life, I saw a definite negative side that overshadowed the positive. We had moved many times, and I never liked the new place, always wanting to go back to the old, to the way things used to be. I was always longing for what was no longer there. I realized I had been running away from something, but I didn't know what.

I attended a ballet in which there was a solo performance. The name of the piece could have been "Despair." When it was finished, I was enveloped in all my negative feelings. I stared into a deep, black, bottomless pit. Where had it come from? Where could I hide? I was terrified, helpless, exposed—and alone once again.

Something was wrong with me. I needed help, but where could I go? I felt I must get away from my family, Dad in particular. I knew he had played a large part in my unhappiness. He was such a negative person. He was so angry all the time. Why did he have such control over me? Why couldn't I be *me* and not feel guilty? I believed I would go to my grave cursing him for ruining my life.

Around this time, I wrote a personal history that included the episodes of the milkman and the ballet. I showed it to my parents. It was the only way I could bring myself to tell them what my feelings were without confronting them openly.

Mom was furious at the milkman. I told her I was upset at her for not preparing me emotionally to handle it. Dad felt really sad about being such an inept father. He told me he hadn't had the easiest childhood either.

I then remembered an incident about his dad, my grandpa. Grandpa had left a horse at a certain spot in the barnyard. He was gone for a while, and she moved a few feet. He was furious when he came back and whipped her for a good five minutes. Maybe his temper had something to do with Dad's—and, I'm sure, mine.

CHAPTER 12

SEARCHING

Shortly after this discussion with my parents, I moved out west, 750 miles away, to one of the wealthier provinces that had natural resources to rely on in order to sustain a higher standard of living. Perhaps I could find my bliss there.

I settled down in an apartment in my new town. I showed my story to my clergyman; he referred me to a psychologist. I didn't like the psychologist. He would ask, "Do you like this or that?" referring to my body and being very specific.

"No, I don't like this or that. No, I don't like my body."

I felt guilty going to see a psychologist. Airing one's problems to others was just not done in the context I grew up in. We believed psychologists didn't know what they were doing, couldn't be trusted, and didn't know the truth (church truth, that is). I quit going.

Since the milkman episode, I had become obsessed with sex. I knew nothing about it, emotionally or physically, other than it was how a girl got pregnant. When I learned about sex at the age of 13 in a biology class, I almost threw up. It was the most revolting idea I'd ever heard. But I was fascinated by it. I wanted to go to a dirty movie just to see what it was like, even though thinking about it made me feel guilty. When I moved, it became easier to delve into such things. Working at a convenience store, I had access to porn magazines, which I read at every opportunity.

I wondered if I was a lesbian, as the female body (in the magazine) turned me on much more than the male body. I started masturbating. I enjoyed looking at and making love, in my mind, to the female body. *But why am I not attracted to women in real life? Maybe I'm a guy trapped in a female body! What do I do now? Who can I talk with about this, if anyone? Am I never going to get this straightened out?*

Church members didn't seem to understand or know how to deal with me.

I started dating a guy, CR. He was also a church member. I fell in love—but what a strange love it seemed to be. I hated him one minute and loved him the next. It didn't seem to matter if I was with him or not. I couldn't explain why, but I knew it had a great deal to do with how I felt about myself. If I felt good that day, then I liked him. If I was depressed, I found myself hating him, focusing on his faults. It was a case of "can't live with him, can't live without him".

Through a course on overcoming self-defeating behaviour, I learned about a cycle I was experiencing. Something would upset me. I would become depressed, masturbate, feel guilty, and go to church. Then I would feel better, feel guilty for feeling good, and become depressed. Then the cycle would repeat.

I began to realize that I used masturbation when faced with a crisis in my life, which seemed to happen all the time. I also used sleep to avoid confronting my problems.

I managed to break the cycle once in a while by thinking of myself as a person of worth, strong enough to overcome it. It worked, sometimes for a few months, but I wasn't able to hang on to it longer. At times I thought I had overcome it for sure, and I became excited about life. Other times I was right back down in the dumps.

At one point I thought I had destroyed my "old self". Joy! The feeling lasted longer than usual, but it still didn't last. I went back to being an emotional teeter-totter, sometimes changing within the hour. (Manic depressive, anyone?)

As CR and I became more involved with each other, I learned many things about me. The more I liked CR, the more I realized how I was treating him when I was upset with myself. It made me realize how hard I was on *me. How do I stop hating myself? How do I forgive? How do I be kind?* I didn't know, and no one else—whether CR, church leaders, or friends—seemed to know either.

My heart said, "I'm in love."

My head said, "He's not worth it."

How could I love someone who didn't deserve my love? My judgment *couldn't* be wrong. I didn't care. I wanted to marry him. How could I get him to propose? Maybe a new dress would do it.

We had first met in 1979 because he was looking for a ballroom dance partner and I loved to dance. After taking some lessons and showing off at church dances, for the next three years we were heavily involved in performing floor shows for church dances.

One summer evening in 1985, we planned to go dancing. I decided to go all out. The new dress was the most expensive dress I'd ever owned, and he really liked it. As the evening wore on, I knew he wasn't going to propose. The more I realized it, the more upset I became. The evening finally ended with me in tears and CR upset because I was upset.

The next day I confronted him: "Here is all your stuff. We're breaking up."

"It's probably for the best," he replied.

I destroyed everything he had given me.

Depression hit me like ocean waves: surging, then retreating. I began to make excuses to see him, hating myself afterwards for being so weak.

I wanted to go back to the farm. For the most part, my memories there were happy ones. I hadn't been back for years and was aching to go. *I'll be happy if only I can get back to it.*

I arranged a short trip, but when I got there, I was still unhappy. Oh, to be the same as I had been when I was a little kid, unencumbered with life's foibles. Weeping, I knew I would never return to that magical time.

When I got back to the house I was renting with friends, I went deeper and deeper into depression. I didn't have anything to go back to. By October, it was all I could do to get through a day's work without breaking down and crying for no reason. After work, I would go to my room and sit on my bed in the dark. Staring at the wall, I rocked and rocked and rocked. Sometimes I cried and sometimes not. I felt empty of all feeling. I was getting to a point of not caring about living any more, and I felt powerless to stop it. I thought, *I must be going crazy.*

One Tuesday in late October, I couldn't get through my workday. I took the afternoon off, went home, and slept—my only refuge.

"What's happening to me?" I asked myself. "I must patch things up with CR. He seems my only hope and reason for living." So I met him at church, where I was to help him with a dance class.

"Please talk to me," I requested. We sat in my car. I tried to explain why I felt so hopeless and helpless, but nothing came out right. He soon left as he didn't know what to say or do.

I felt despair. I was alone, so alone. So horribly alone.

The car engine was running. The car faced a brick building, which seemed to beckon to me. *Why not end it all?* I wondered. *Why not end the pain, the depression, the suffering?* Sobbing, almost screaming, riveted to my seat, I fought to keep my hands off the wheel. I knew if I touched that wheel, I would drive straight into that wall. Hours later, or so it seemed, I was exhausted, spent. *I just want to go home.*

The next day, I was on top of the world. "I am *happy*!" I declared. "I'm finally over CR." It certainly seemed so. I couldn't feel anything for him. No depression!

I got on with my life. Church demanded a lot of time and energy, and that's what I put into it. Everything was going great until Christmas, when I went to a church dance and saw CR. Dance had brought us together, and I was glad to see him because I knew I'd have a great dance partner.

The dance started out being a lot of fun, like the good old days. The music was particularly good, and we were dancing well. I was feeling great. Slowly, slowly the old feelings of being in love crept back in. *No, it can't be. I thought I was over him.*

CR didn't help. In fact, he had been quite uncharacteristic all evening, asking specifically if I was with anyone, complimenting me on my dress, and so on. I didn't know where he was coming from. Depression hit once again.

Moving to my own apartment was a good diversion. I fell in love with my private space and devoted my time to making it into a little home.

Because the move took me out of the church boundary, I lost the church job I had been putting all my time and energy into. I now had nothing to do. It was weird. I had no feelings for anything. Even though I was upset at losing my church job, I really didn't care. The only thing I cared about was my work.

Because I didn't seem to care about anything, I couldn't be bothered with anything. Before Christmas, I had been taking a religion class. After the move, I found I had no more interest in it and even felt a definite pull away from it.

At the same time, I had been involved in singing Handel's *Messiah*. I continued only because I felt I would regret it later if I didn't. I ended up thoroughly enjoying it.

When asked to participate in church in my new area, I flatly refused. I felt that it would be too much of a strain on me. Yet I couldn't feel anything, negative *or* positive. I seemed to be living totally and completely on the surface, something I had never done before.

In April, three months after my move, I attended a church conference telecast from the States. For

Jennifer Gross

the first time in many months, I saw the president of the church there. Normally I'd have a warm, peaceful feeling whenever I saw him, but that day there was nothing. I used to tingle all over when I knew someone was speaking with the Spirit. Again, that day there was nothing.

Why? Why couldn't I feel? What was wrong? Even those questions seemed too much for me to give my time and energy to. So I didn't.

CHAPTER 13

AWAKENING

For the first time in my life, I went on a diet program. I was fine for two weeks, but then started snitching here and there. I yo-yoed back and forth until my counsellor said I wasn't ready to commit to the diet and took me off. "Why can't I stay on the diet? Why don't I want to?" I cried.

After some thought, I realized I didn't *want* to become slim and attractive. I didn't know why, other than it was a hang-up and I didn't want to deal with my hang-ups right then.

Meanwhile, a former roommate gave me three books to read. Two dealt with diets and what happened to people who went on them. The third was about happiness. I hadn't realized how closely related dieting and hang-ups were. I soon found out.

After reading Eda LeShan's book *Winning the Losing Battle: Why I'll Never Be Fat Again*, I sat stunned. *I have to change my attitude and feelings about myself? I have to love myself fat? I have used food to solve all my life's problems? I stay fat because I hate myself? I always deny myself self-love?* All of these insights started to make sense when I analysed my life. I responded especially when LeShan talked about how angry we become for wasting our time and efforts on trying to please everyone but ourselves. Perhaps it was true that I was afraid of being thin because then I would have to stop hating myself. I had another reason for staying fat: men would not find me attractive!

I read *How to Be Your Own Best Friend* by Bernhard Berkowitz, Jean Owen, and Mildred Newman. I sobbed all the way through. It talked about happiness and how happiness has to come from within.

I don't think I have it within myself to be happy, I thought. *I know I'm not happy the way I am. I want happiness so badly, but I don't know how to get it from within.* Perhaps that was why one of my favourite Scripture passages had always been, "Love thy neighbour as thyself" (Matt. 22:39 KJV). How could I love my neighbour if I didn't love myself first? How did I do that? Not being able to answer these questions I headed for bed. It was around midnight of 26 May 1984 and I was 32 years old.

As I sat on my bed, I asked, "God, *please*, what is wrong with me?"

My scariest thoughts were *What kind of person is the real me? Am I a whore? Am I really supposed to be a boy? Am I gay? Am I irresponsible? Am I one who really likes being mean and hurtful? Am I a psychopath who has no feelings? Will I like me? Will I love me?*

A few minutes passed. Random thoughts started entering my mind, accompanied by a powerful feeling of truthfulness. They were:

- You became a boy to please your dad.
- Who do little boys want to be like when they grow up? Their dads!
- You actually became your dad!

After the first thought came through, I started to cry. By the time the last one surfaced, I was sobbing uncontrollably. Tightening every muscle in my body, clenching my fists, I opened my mouth to scream out all my frustrations. I felt a tremendous force rise within me, starting from my toes and soaring to my head, pulling away from every cell in my body.

Then I thought, *Don't you dare scream or all the tenants in the building will be pounding on your door, wondering what's happening.* I closed my mouth and started swallowing, trying to stuff the feeling back down.

No! You have to let it out! So I opened my mouth again. With all muscles straining, I pushed with everything I had. "It" came up and out of me.

The sensation only lasted a few minutes, but when the feeling was gone, I couldn't quit shaking. I grabbed hold of myself and thought, *I'm not my dad. I'm not my dad! I'm* me*! And I'm* female*!*

I felt myself all over, and yes, I was a *girl.* I felt relief, even ecstasy. I was overjoyed, thrilled. In that instant, I somehow knew the war was over. Sublime peacefulness flowed into and over me. *Thank you God.*

My memory then went black.

I was a blank: no feelings, no memory of anything other than the fact that I was 32 years old and sitting on a bed—a person with no past.

After what seemed like forever, in the blackness of my mind, I noticed a tiny light moving slowly toward me. As it grew larger, it turned into a picture of a boy. I recognized my brother. *I have a brother!* I thought. Then a picture of a sister came forward, then another sister, until all my siblings had appeared. Then my mom, and last of all, Dad. I had a family!

"I love my dad," I said. For the first time in my life, I knew I loved him. I could love. I'd always had doubts. I could have a man-woman relationship. What a relief!

After these revelations, my first impulses were to phone Dad and tell him I loved him, phone the ex-roommate who had lent me the books and tell her what had happened, give CR a hug *as a female*, write it all down in my journal, clean house, and *sleep*. I opted to clean house and sleep.

It took me two hours to clean, and I hopped into bed around two thirty in the morning. My mind raced with discovery after discovery as to my life's behavioural patterns.

∽ CHAPTER 14 ∽

ENLIGHTENMENT

I had become a boy because it had been expected of me.

Mom used to say that, before I was born, she was sure I was going to be an athlete because I was so active in her womb. Dad had always hoped for boys for a football or baseball team. I became a boy to please my dad. I was always his little helper.

Many a time, Dad and I went to milk cows. (I just watched.) We'd work in the garden side by side. I helped in the hayfields during harvest, picking up bales and so forth.

I had always looked upon my farm experience as the happiest time in my life, though now I realized it was because I'd had no reason to doubt that I was a boy. I had no major inner conflicts until puberty hit. The first three years of a child's life are the most important in forming who the child is. I had been my father's only son for my first five years.

It made sense that my brother was my favourite member of the family, that I had become an older brother to him. No wonder it bothered me so much when he wasn't allowed to be included in some aspects of my life. After all, wasn't I a boy too?

All my life I'd tried to be one of the boys because that's where I felt the most comfortable. Until I was 15, I managed to fool myself to a certain degree. Then I met the milkman.

That was about as far as my thinking got me on that first night, other than, *This sure is cheaper than going to a psychologist!*

I awoke Sunday morning excited to catch my ex-roommate at church and tell her about my news. She wasn't there, and I was quite disappointed. But other people commented that somehow I seemed different. It was a nice validation.

CR and I had started seeing each other again a few weeks prior to this experience. He was coming over for lunch after church that day. Because this had happened the night before and cell phones hadn't been invented yet, I had no way of warning him. I dropped the bomb while we were eating lunch. I'd never seen such a look of concentration on his face as he tried valiantly to understand. After a while, he said it made some sense.

His purpose in coming over was to give me a belated birthday gift. It was a black statue of a rearing horse. What a beautiful gift on such a beautiful day—a gift to the new and very much improved *me*.

CR and I started to fool around and got into some heavy petting. Doing it for the first time as a total female was wonderful. I wanted it to go on all night.

I was extremely tired at work the next day, so exhausted that I couldn't even drink water without feeling like I was going to upchuck. I finally got a glass of water into me around two o'clock. The only thing my mind reacted to was thinking about what CR and I had done the previous evening. I got hot sexually. I wondered why until I realized my body was reacting in a heterosexually feminine way for the first time!

As I stumbled around on Monday and Tuesday, trying to wake up, I realized I had no sense of right and wrong, particularly in connection with CR and me. My feeling was "It's not the right time. It's too soon." Perhaps I just needed time to think about my experience of Saturday night and what it all meant.

Later I came to realize that somehow I had gone back to an infant stage of not knowing anything about morals. I couldn't connect with having lived before. I was only interested in food, sleep, and affection.

I walked around my apartment with nothing on, just so I could see myself in the mirror and once again realize I was a female.

With this "no morals" perspective, I was willing to let CR give me all the affection he could. I tried to persuade him to give it to me in the form of sex. I realized I had absolutely no qualms about going into a store and buying birth control items. In fact, I was eagerly looking forward to having sex.

But sometime between Tuesday night and Friday, I had a different thought. *Why do something you will only have to repent of later? Why go through all that pain and suffering if you don't need to?* So I didn't buy anything.

Then I thought, *Why do I know I'll repent later on?*

On Thursday I wrote in my journal:

Many, many insights have come to me since that Saturday night. I'm trying to remember them all and I may eventually do so. But it seems I think of at least two or three a day, get tired and can't remember what they were.

I'm quite wrapped up in finding out who me is. I literally do not know what I think about anything in life because I don't know anything about the real me. It's exciting but also extremely tiring. I seem to be able to concentrate and comprehend for only four or five hours at a time. I am only able to hang on to an idea for maybe five minutes. If I don't write it down, it's lost for two or three days. I then feel an intense need to sleep just like a newborn who needs lots of sleep as they begin to discover the world around them.

I have no interest whatever in current world affairs, my work, the church, etc. I don't really know what I want, or what I'm interested in. I have stopped getting the paper till I grow up a little more. I feel that these are decisions I just have no power to cope with. Decisions to be made in the future. I feel I have to go through every stage of my life all over again to discover who I am, because I was never allowed to do so as a child. Right now if I want to do something, I'll do it. If I don't, I won't. I'm interested mainly in finding out what foods I like, what I can do to make my apartment the way I really want it. My whole attitude seems to be totally and purely selfish. I'm experimenting with new foods. I'm interested in surrounding myself with things that reflect me and only me. I am excited about discovering the world around me and what the real me likes and dislikes. With shapes, I prefer round and oval to square or blunt edges. I like bright cheery colours, blues, greens, yellows, oranges and RED! I want some kid's toys to play with, kid books to read, kid rides at parks and so forth.

I hate my waterbed frame. It doesn't have rounded corners thus looking too masculine.

I want a car with an automatic instead of my standard shift.

I feel weak physically. I don't have to fool myself into thinking I need to be physically superior. I am curious about things, which means I can learn! It is exhilarating as I never thought I had any brains. My first sunrise and rainbow were absolutely thrilling. I saw them from my front room window. All I could do was stand and stare and drink them in.

On Friday, less than a week after my incident, CR and I saw a movie. It was my first date! It was really nice to have him ask me out and pay for everything. Afterwards at my place, we sat and talked for a couple of hours, cuddling each other in a big chair. It was lovely. We talked about many things.

I told him I loved him because during the past week I had just found out. Not only was it news to him, it was news to me also. I had wondered time and again if I loved him. Because I'd been so up and down all the time, he had wondered too. Before, I couldn't look at his faults without becoming very irritated. Now I had no feelings concerning his faults, other than knowing he had them. I could *accept* him *as he was*! I no longer feel guilty about loving someone who wasn't perfect—which in my mind meant they weren't going to create conflict.

CR opened up that night and told me how he really felt about many things. After six years of association he was finally telling me. It was wonderful.

Previously in our relationship, I had done, or tried to do, all the "male" things. I had asked him out. I had wanted to handle the finances if we married. I had been trying to be the spiritual leader. I liked cars, sports, and working outside.

I had wanted CR to be the emotional strength of the two of us, to be the peacemaker, to be the quiet one. I had wanted him to be nonconfrontational, even submissive. I had wanted him to play the female role—or what I thought to be the female role. He always refused, though at the time he didn't know it, and I had hated him for it. He never knew where he stood with me because I was hot one minute and cold the next. This was probably because the female part of me would surface every once in a while, and I could accept him and love him despite his faults.

Sometime during that first week of understanding, two impressions hit me. First, I was a little blonde girl, innocent and undefiled. Second, if I had not accepted the male role, I would have accepted the church and its teachings without hesitation or rebellion. A great feeling of sadness came over me as I realized how different my life would have been. I thought, *I do not have a rebellious or negative spirit! I can now accept church assignments willingly, eagerly, and cheerfully.* This was the opposite of how I used to feel.

By the end of that first week, I felt I had to tell Dad what had happened to me. I had been putting it off for as long as possible, for fear he wouldn't accept this very strange experience as truth. All his life, he had been a seeker of truth.

CHAPTER 15

DAD'S LETTER

I finally wrote him a letter on Sunday morning, 3 June 1984, relating how I had found out I was a girl, not a boy.

I now look at myself as a child and as a child I have absolutely no sense of moral values. To me there is no right or wrong. Words like selfish, kind, obedience, and faith seem to have no meaning for me. I wondered about that. I thought "Now that I'm a child and will have to learn from the beginning, who will be my teacher? Who can I trust to teach me exactly what I need to know in order to grow up being me? I at first thought of CR but realized that if I did that, I would only grow away from him as I "got older" as the normal parent-child relationship took its course. Then I thought "Why don't you choose someone who is already a parent and who knows a lot about it?" The only person I could think of, who qualified, was the Lord.

Now I know what the teachings of the Lord are: go to church, pray, read the scriptures. So although I have no 'feeling' for these things, I have decided I will do them because that is what the Lord has already laid out in his plan. I don't know they are true as yet. It seems I have to gain a testimony all over again. It seems my male self had a testimony and a very strong testimony it was too. But I feel now that I have nothing, that I am literally starting from the beginning.

My first thought, after deciding to go to church, was about going to the adult Sunday School class. My reaction was a very definite "NO!" Do you know where I'd like to go? To the children's classes! Then I thought, "Well, maybe I should teach the class." Again there was a "No!" I finally realized I wanted to go as one of the three year olds. To sit and learn as a child! Since I think the teacher will be most uncomfortable having an adult in her class as a student, I'm going to check out the manual from the library and read it during that time. I know all this must sound crazy to you but I'm EXCITED about starting at the very beginning and LEARNING because it will be a whole new me who's doing it.

Now to go back to what happened last October when I decided to live. I was discussing my discovery about myself with a friend and former roommate and how I had been feeling, or not feeling, from October to May. She said I had internalized the struggle. I was no longer "lashing out" to those around me as I have done these past ten or fifteen years. I had brought that struggle totally within myself. Because I was struggling so hard with all I had, I had absolutely nothing left over to feel for anyone or anything else. I realized this was true the following day. The thought struck me that it had been the "real" me who had decided to live that October night. But in order for the real me to live, it was necessary for me to get rid of the unreal me. And thus the process was started which finally came to a head last Saturday night. "It was an immense relief to discover I wasn't you and I wasn't a boy."

Looking back at my first "sexual encounter" I now realize why it was so devastating to me. I was looking at it as a boy, thus, instead of it being a male-female encounter, it was a male-male or homosexual encounter for me. That was why I constantly thought suicide for the following year and I let it ruin my life for so long and why whenever a man would look at me, I could only see a male-male encounter. Do you see now why I'm not married and don't have children? How could I when I thought I was a man!

I haven't really begun to think about why I liked certain family members and why I seemed to hate others so much, yourself included. With you, I think it was a matter of my male self wanting to be like you and my female self knowing I couldn't so it was a constant inner war. All through my life, I've known you had a major part in what was making me so unhappy. I don't blame you or anyone, least of all me, for the anger I felt. I can't blame anyone. I honestly tried to fill a role that, at first, was expected of me or at least, was wanted of me. With a child's heart, I did it, knowing subconsciously all along that it wasn't really me.

It's exciting to do things I've never done before. I feel I have never lived before now. I cannot relate at all to my 'former' life. I know I went through those experiences because I have written them down. Every day is new and exciting and I want to live it because I will have discovered something about myself I didn't know before.

So, my dear loving Dad, I leave you with much to think about, to ponder over.

I love you. I can't find it in my heart to blame you. Al I can do is ask for your forgiveness in hating you so much. I know my hate and anger have hurt you so many times.

I only hope this letter has given you an insight into why. I sit here and cry with happiness that these revelations have come to me at a time when you're still here on the earth and I can share them with you.

When writing my letter to Dad, I spoke of the milkman experience, so I reread it in my personal history. As I did so, I reacted to it as if for the first time, as *female*. I cried and cried as I relived it. I have since concluded that when I feel ready, I will have to go over my whole history and relive it as the real me. Only then will I feel I have actually lived before now. Only then will I be able to reconnect myself to my previous experiences.

CHAPTER 16

INSIGHTS

After finishing Dad's letter, I started getting ready for church. How I wished I had something lacy or frilly to wear. I wanted a bow in my hair, cute earrings—anything to tell the world I was a *girl*. I wore the most feminine thing I could find, but it just wasn't enough.

While in church, all I wanted to do was hang my legs over the end of a pew and swing them. I was totally disinterested in the talks. I looked at all the babes in arms and felt like I was one of them.

After the meeting, I checked out the lessons for 3-year-olds and read the first one. The teacher was supposed to greet each child by name and say something about them, such as "This is so-and-so who is smiling" and so forth. I chose "This is Miriam, who is a pretty girl." I learned that I was "three years old", though that age felt too old. I felt good and warm inside. I was going to learn about Heavenly Father and do new and fun things. That made me even happier. "Happy three year old!" the lesson said. Yes, I was a happy 3-year-old!

Lesson two said that we each had a family. Heavenly Father had placed each one of us in a family. Families might be made up of fathers, mothers, brothers, and sisters. The lesson urged me to think of myself as happy to belong to a family. I couldn't identify with this lesson at all. I felt very vague about it.

Lesson three had the theme "How does my family show that I am important to them?" It was as far as I got with that lesson. Even though I remembered that Mom and Dad had called me on my birthday two weeks before my change, I had been upset with what they'd had to say: "What are you doing church-wise? Are there any guys around?" I hadn't been interested in talking to them about that. But I hadn't felt I could tell them so, as they'd jump down my throat about it. I had been thrilled they had called because they rarely did, but I didn't need their comments. I kept reminding myself, "It's the thought that counts."

After reading the church lessons, I told my clergyman about all this. He was quite excited for me. It was nice that he seemed to understand. He then asked, "What would you like to do in the church?" I came up blank. I couldn't relate to that notion at all. So much for his understanding.

During the next week, more insights came:

I always wondered how members could marry Non-members and make love to them if they didn't believe the same way? I realized I could marry CR (who is not very active) and be very happy because: 1. I'm happy with myself. 2. I love him and 3. I don't need him to make me happy. I used to think, "Oh, if only some guy would come along and make me happy." I no longer think that way.

When my brother was born, I resented him to a certain degree and now believe it was because he was a 'real' boy and was treated differently.

One of the ways I tried to be like Dad was to get into accounting. He was good at it. I was disappointed to find I was not.

At church, I always wanted to go to the men's meetings as I felt I belonged there more than at the women's organization.

My mission was confusing. I agreed to go not only because I had been taught to be extremely obedient (most important thing you can do in the church, besides gain a testimony of the divinity of Christ), but because men are expected to go. It felt wonderful to be among all those men, but not allowed to become buddies.

Guilt overrode everything I did. I couldn't trust anyone for answers even though I was always asking why. Fear of finding out what I was really like was a major problem. I was terrified of change. I liked anything about the past. I liked history and hated Science: Fact or Fiction, computers, high tech.

I was into conveniences: a wallet instead of a purse (easier to carry). Stereotypical guy?

During the week, I bought some kids' books— colouring, math, dot to dot, storybooks—and worked in them every day. Because my handwriting looked too grown-up, I did everything with my left hand, which was non dominant. I redecorated my apartment in early childhood imagery by putting up pictures of nursery rhyme characters, baby animals, and raindrops. I bought flannel board figures of a family. I moved my kitchen table and chairs into the spare room and used my coffee table as my kitchen table. I borrowed two kiddie chairs from a friend to sit on. It felt just right! I borrowed a tape of children's church songs and played it constantly. My apartment became a haven against the unreal grown-up world just outside my door.

CHAPTER 17

RELIVING AGES 0 TO 1YR

During that first week, I felt a great need to bake something, anything. Yet when I did, I found I hardly ate any of it. Previously, whenever I was in a new situation in my life, I had baked. Somehow, I felt more secure after baking. Since that first week, I have not felt like baking, regardless of my changing situations. I only do it when my freezer is getting empty.

I discussed this experience with CR and three former roommates over the next two weeks. Each reacted differently. CR was affectionate. One roommate responded intellectually and analytically, a second with lots of emotion, and the last one by invoking the spiritual aspect. I felt the least drained, emotionally and physically, after talking about the spiritual aspect. I love teddy bears. I used to have a five-footer I'd snuggle with, but he now felt too big. My spiritual roommate gave me a little seven-inch one, and he was just right for the longest time.

I started my period during the second week and got the shock of my life. For the first few days, whenever I'd get ready to insert a tampon, my gut reaction was "It's too *big*! It's not going to fit!" I had to continually tell myself, "It's OK. It'll fit."

Along with experimenting with food, I bread binged. I couldn't seem to get enough. I also craved sleep. I slept a solid eight or ten hours a night for the first week. Then I began to sleep for shorter periods and get more tired more often. All I wanted to do when I was awake was eat, eat, and eat some more. I put on weight and couldn't regard it as fat.

Within the first few weeks, I realized that *I had gone back to the infant stage of life.* I was reliving my entire emotional life all over again but *as a female*, starting straight from the womb. I had a period of darkness, of not knowing who or what I was. I just wanted to eat and sleep like a newborn. Because I had never been a milk drinker and I loved bread, bread was like milk to me.

I got my time clues from going to church. My first week, I gravitated to babies, something I had never done much of in my life. About the fourth or fifth week, I again wanted to swing my legs over the side of the pew. Sermons held no interest for me, whereas before I had judged like crazy the content of anyone's speech. It was at that time I realized I was living a year of emotional life in a week of real time, i.e., at the end of the first week, I was like a 1-year-old.

> I can only tolerate classical, easy-listening, children's or church music. I can tolerate anything else for about 15 seconds at the most. I wonder if it had to do with the kind of music that was played at home when I was young.
>
> I can say yes and I can say no. I never felt able to say no to anyone before. I always aimed to please and keep the peace, so I never said no.
>
> Both my female and male selves were in love with the spiritual roommate so there was no inner conflict regarding her as there was with every other roommate.
>
> I discovered I absolutely love taking showers instead of baths and I almost don't

need an excuse to take one. If the idea hits, no matter what I'm doing, I'll just do it. Baths were the me that was trying to forget I had a female body. A friend said, "Taking a shower requires one to pay attention to what you are doing".

I feel I trust everyone as a child does. I do not judge anyone. I can accept the fact that everyone has faults and it no longer bothers me. I still find I dislike some people, though I don't know why.

I'm just like a little kid. I need a parent around to remind me to pray, read the scriptures, turn out the light, etc. I see the value of having someone physically around to "guide" me to do wholesome things, like having a schedule for eating, sleeping, and playing.

One day at work, a song came on the radio. It was the Beatles' "Yesterday". When they sang, "I'm not half the man I used to be", I just cracked up, laughing so hard I almost cried. *Thank goodness!* I thought.

I realized how my male self had dominated in the music department. I had learned the tenor part of most hymns, convincing myself it was the prettiest.

One night I wanted to do something adult really badly, so I got a pizza and watched TV for an hour and a half. It was kinda fun.

There was a change in the church clergy, and I told the new clergyman about my experience. He said I shouldn't stay in one phase too long, using it as a cop-out so I didn't have to progress. I worried about that, but looking back over my life, I couldn't see where, in all my struggling, I had ever copped out on the church. I had worked in every organization and in almost every position open to women in the church, from counsellor to secretary to teacher to music director to librarian.

CHAPTER 18

RELIVING AGES 2YRS TO 3YRS

In week two, I went to church. Many thoughts hit me during the meeting. "Ye shall know the truth and the truth shall make you free," (John 8:22 KJV). I paraphrased it: You shall know the truth about yourself and God and the truth shall set you free, free to BE the REAL YOU! Working through and getting rid of hang ups and becoming the real me is the only way to become more God like.I am no longer hung up about being perfect. I don't "dread" judgment day because the choices I make are mine and I take full responsibility for them.

One of the speakers spoke on the Spirit of Truth and how it speaks peace to one's mind. I thought, "What greater witness can I have about what I have just experienced?" The truth about me had been spoken to my mind and had given me great peace—so great that it filled my whole being.

After church, I tackled the children's lessons again. The next one had the theme "I love my father". I couldn't relate. I read the lesson and had no feelings at all. I didn't want to bring back all the negative feelings I'd had and try to work through them.

A thought came: *Think of yourself as a child and then think of your father.* When I did, I saw a pretty little blonde girl following her daddy all around because she loved him so much. A wonderfully warm feeling came over me. I had become a boy because I loved my daddy so much and wanted to please him.

I moved on to the next couple of lessons which were about mothers and brothers. I didn't feel a thing. I had a very vague image of Mom. Nothing specific had happened in my childhood that brought her to the front of my memory, other than when she made us finish those dratted dishes or let us play much longer than we were supposed to. Because I couldn't relate to the lessons, I left them awhile.

I wrote in my journal until I didn't feel like writing any more. It hit me how neat it was to be able to go from one thing to another and just quit when I didn't feel like doing it. Previously, I had been used to scheduling activities by time alone. It was an entirely new feeling to start and stop when I wanted to.

I thought about taking time off work just to give myself a break from feeling exhausted all the time. I asked CR for a loan to cover expenses while I took a few days off. I was self-employed, so I had no paid vacations and no money saved. He readily agreed, which shocked me. I realized what a good guy he was.

I ecstatically went about my workday, planning all the fun places I would go during my time off: an amusement park, the zoo, a heritage park that highlighted farm life, a riding stable. I also planned to buy books, records, and toys.

The next Sunday, I discovered that a child could become super frustrated and have an awfully bad day. All they needed was an understanding moment with someone. I had the frustration but no understanding someone.

I was 3 years old emotionally. CR was coming over for lunch as my guinea pig for new recipes. I thought I had bought everything I needed, but I realized late on Saturday night that I was missing a couple of things. I went to the store on Sunday. For religious reasons, I rarely shopped on Sundays. I felt terrible. That was my first frustration. The second was that I went to church but had no feelings about anything. The third was that I walked home from church and saw CR on his way over. Yet when I reached my place, he was nowhere to be found.

The frustrations kept coming. The fourth was that I slaved for two hours preparing dinner, expecting CR at any minute. The fifth was that, because I was so tired, I went to bed for an hour. When I awoke, CR still hadn't shown up, so I called him. He had come over and gotten no answer to his knock. He left for ten minutes, came back, and still found no one. He went home, planning to call me when he got there. But he *forgot*!

Thus, my sixth frustration was eating a cold supper alone. Just as I was finishing, church visitors knocked on my door. The seventh was having to listen to their lesson, "Enduring to the End." One of them asked me, "How do you *feel* about enduring to the end?"

I was taken aback. I didn't feel anything for any principle of the church. I felt like asking her, "What do you expect a 3-year-old to feel?" Instead I tried to give an adult answer. The more I tried, the worse it got. I probably wasn't making any sense, and I just got more frustrated. They asked what they could do for me, and I said, "Just let me be", meaning to give me time to be a little child and for them to respond to me as a child. But I was so angry and frustrated that nothing was coming out right. So I left it at that. It took my questioner by surprise, as she didn't know and couldn't understand where I was coming from.

After the church visitors left, I sat thinking about my feelings. I had been a typical child when trying to answer the question. My questioner had expected an answer, and even though I had none to give her, I had tried. I wanted to please her. I could talk about theories and ideas till I was blue in the face, but I didn't seem to have any feelings on any subject.

A former roommate phoned and asked that I give the closing prayer at her mission farewell church meeting. I cleaned house for hours, trying not to get too nervous. Sunday, 24 June, finally arrived, and I awoke feeling awful. My stomach was in knots. *You'll be fine, you'll be fine*, I told myself. *Three-year-olds can pray.*

I tried to give an adult prayer. I should have given a child's one instead. When I got home, I still felt sick, so I went to bed. Upon arising, I felt better. I realized I had had the same reaction in previous years; I got sick, to the point of throwing up, if I had to stand before a crowd, though usually I had been performing a song and not speaking.

I watched movies that felt just right: *Dumbo, Babes in Toyland,* and *Tale of Two Critters.* The real me loved animals—horses in particular—and dance. Those loves had carried over from my former life.

I found it exhilarating, comforting, and relief-giving to be surrounded by people who loved me and accepted my change.

CHAPTER 19

RELIVING AGES 4YRS TO 6 YRS

I worked every other day for two weeks. My days off were strictly for being a kid. One day I went horseback riding and worked in my kid books. Another day I worked on church books. I had borrowed a set of books from church which were designed for children. One passage from the Book of Mormon grabbed my attention: "And blessed art thou, Nephi, because thou believest in the Son of the most high God; wherefore, thou shalt behold the things which thou has desired" (1 Nephi 11:6). I felt the Lord was speaking directly to me. I took out a transcript of a blessing which had been given to me and reread it. I was impressed with the idea that I had a specific mission to perform here on earth. Strains of "Bless This House" were playing in the background. A beautiful, peaceful feeling pervaded the room, as if the Lord was blessing my apartment, my little home.

The next day, I turned on the TV for the first time in weeks (I was about 6 years old) and saw a woman being chased by someone in a car on some cop show. She fell on top of the hood and smashed against the windshield, smearing blood all over it. I felt a stab of pain go through me and instantly became sick to my stomach. I found I couldn't stand violence of any kind. During that same week, I saw a documentary on China about birth control by sterilization. *"No, it's wrong!"* I cried. I was starting to have opinions.

Two days later, I took a client's kids, boys ages 4 and 6, to an amusement park. I had a riot. It was quite interesting to observe them. They were extremely shy to begin with, but after I persuaded them to try a couple of things, they were off and running. We had a great day. We drank when we got thirsty and ate when we got hungry. I had to drag one of them with us when his brother and I had had enough. My only disappointment was not being able to do many of the things they did. Many of the rides wouldn't accommodate me as an adult. I was too big! When we got back to their home, we discovered we'd been together for *six hours!* It was the most fun I'd had in the whole two weeks of my vacation, with the exception of horseback riding.

That afternoon, I found Dad's answer to my letter in the mailbox. I went upstairs, opened it, read it, and cried. I couldn't understand why he said what he did. He mentioned my letter three times. Just three sentences out of a letter that was four foolscap pages long. Not one feeling was expressed. All he talked about was the "gospel plan". I couldn't relate what he said to *anything* I had written.

I came away feeling that, though he had fathered my earthly body, he was not my father. He hadn't reacted the way I so wanted him to react: as a kind, loving father, one who at least could say, "I don't understand what you were talking about, but I love you regardless." When I finished reading the letter, I was very sad. I didn't have a father; he was dead to me.

I was mad at him for two full days, flying into an absolute rage whenever I thought of him and his letter. It was a temper tantrum. I decided to tell him exactly what and how I felt and thought.

Calming down, I was ultimately able to respond with much less anger in my tone and far fewer swear words. And I didn't send it. It was a relief to find out I wasn't him, as he couldn't communicate his feelings. I could and I did. I would fight for him and with him. I would keep after him until he opened up.

I literally forced myself to read his letter a second time in hopes of finding something to relate to, but again I couldn't. I experienced the same sad feeling. Colouring was my only escape that night.

By Sunday, the anger had been replaced with a wonderful feeling of being alive. I knew I could respond to Dad's letter in a relatively sensible manner.

I wrote him another letter. I told him just how his letter had made me feel. I asked him never to talk to me like that again. *Don't treat me as the unreal me. I will not stand for it.*

Saturday, I spent five hours at the zoo with a former roommate. It was great fun. I was disappointed, though, with the lack of little animals for me to pet. That had been a major reason I wanted to go. I wanted to touch some animals.

Looking back on my weight problem, I realized it might have been a reaction to trying to be male. Men are usually bigger and stronger. I became bigger and stronger, at least more so than any member of my family. Most everyone else, my brother included, was at or very near their ideal weight.

I talked with the gal who had given me the diet books about Dad's reaction to my letter. I expressed particular frustration about the way Dad tried to fit everything into church mode and had no interest if he couldn't. She mentioned that I reacted to CR that way. In fact, I reacted that way towards everyone.

On further reflection, I wondered why CR was letting me treat him that way. I decided he was *gutless*. Dad had treated me like that once, and I had refused to let him get away with it. CR hadn't put up a fight in the six years I had treated him like that. I was in love with a wimp!

CR disagreed. He said he hadn't stood up to me because he was afraid of what I might do. He would tell me something and I'd be depressed for days, so he was always afraid to say anything.

One evening I took him completely by surprise. He was talking about his model airplanes and how he never talked about them because most people weren't interested in that sort of thing. I asked him to explain a little about them, such as how the flaps worked, the tail section, and so forth—in short, the principles of aerodynamics. "Work my mind," I told him. He was quite thrilled to do so.

He came over for Sunday dinner and later told me he wanted to cut out the "fun" stuff we'd been engaging in. He said the proper emotions just weren't there. I agreed and then started crying. I couldn't understand why; I just had to cry. I then realized it might be a childish reaction. I was still 6 years old emotionally. If something was taken away, I would cry.

I was learning to identify different emotions. Thrilling. Before, it seemed I could only feel depression. Now I could feel sad, unhappy, and confused, but I felt hardly any depression and no guilt. Truly amazing!

CHAPTER 20

RELIVING AGES 7YRS TO 12YRS

I was just turning 7 emotionally when one of my older sisters arrived in town as part of a trip into the Canadian Rockies. She didn't believe what was happening to me, in terms of going back to my childhood emotionally, but she was open to the fact that I had changed. She felt I was doing the same thing she had done years ago: examining everything she had been taught, deciding what she was going to believe, and throwing the rest out. She had created her personal standard for living. We had a fun time together, but I found it tiring to talk on an adult level for very long.

My sister invited me to visit her in the States to see the bus she and her husband had spent the last three years renovating. The more I thought about going, the better I liked the idea. I decided to go during Labour Day weekend in September. Seeing the bus didn't seem to be my reason for going, but I didn't know what the reason was until I figured out how "old" I would be then. I would be turning 13, which had been my age when we moved to the States to live with my mom's mom.

Between the emotional ages of about 4 and 8, I had an almost overwhelming desire to try things that were the no-nos of the church—cigarettes, coffee, beer, and sex—just out of curiosity.

As I approached the age of 8, I was waiting for a great religious feeling to come over me: a tingling in my soul, warm feeling, and so forth. I had been baptized at 8 years old. Church doctrine said that Satan could not tempt a child before the age of 8. After that, you become responsible for your actions.

I didn't experience any feelings, but those desires for the forbidden disappeared within a twenty-four-hour period. I wasn't interested in pornography anymore. I felt I could wait till marriage before having sex. It was a relief not always having sex on my mind.

The Summer Olympics started the week I turned 8. I was fascinated. I couldn't seem to see or hear enough of the events. I drank them up.

It was as if I was watching the Olympics for the first time. Because of the excellent TV coverage of most events, I was introduced to some I didn't even know existed. Previously, I had stuck to certain ones. This time around, I found myself watching everything, even boxing, which used to be at the bottom of my list. I had a great desire to learn everything I could about all the sports.

Around this time, I heard that a friend was looking for a place to rent for a few months. At first I thought of letting her rent with me. Then I thought, *Too young. You're too young to handle having someone else around just yet.*

A week or so later, I decided she could move in while I was on my trip to the US, when I would be 13 emotionally. The only problem was I had to redecorate my apartment in an older style, bringing back the adult-size table and chairs, for one thing. *That's too old! I want my kiddie chairs back.* I didn't eat in the kitchen for a couple of weeks, as it felt so strange.

I let my friend read Dad's letter and found out she was coming to similar conclusions as to who and what she had been all her life. She fit right in.

I received a letter from another sister in the States, who said she was anxiously awaiting my arrival. I hadn't planned on visiting her. I didn't know how she found out I was coming. I didn't think she would understand what I had gone through and I didn't want to see her. I still couldn't handle being around people whom I thought couldn't understand. The letter bothered me to the extent I started feeling sick and I didn't want to go. I thought, *I am not going to let you stop me. I've got to go.*

I wanted CR to come along to help drive—the trip would take about fifteen hours. I realized he had become my emotional pillar of strength. He had also become a bit of a father figure. Dad had been emotionally unstable, and CR was the exact opposite. I wanted CR around when I relived that part of my life. He was quite willing to go when I explained why.

CHAPTER 21

RELIVING AGES 13YRS TO 22YRS

On 30 August 1984, CR and I left for the States. I was just turning 13. In the States, I was able to visit the sites of many old memories: high school, church, and the neighbourhood. I also saw the most important people I'd had as friends: my second parents and a high school religion teacher. I told them what was happening in my life and found them to be very supportive and happy for me. My teacher gave me the idea of writing this book.

When visiting the sister I hadn't wanted to see, she told me that I hadn't become like Dad, but like what I had perceived him to be. Didn't all kids relate to what they perceived as truth?

On the way home, I got a crush on CR. The feeling hit just out of the blue. I like him much more than a friend. I cried and didn't know what to do. Since the feeling hit just before we turned in for the night—we camped on the way—he said, "Let's talk about it in the morning." I turned over and immediately fell asleep. I slept straight through for nine or ten hours! It was the longest sleep I'd had in a long, long time.

When I awoke, I was facing the tent wall. My moving around indicated I was awake, and CR asked, "How are you?"

"Fine."

It was very hard to bring myself to turn around and face him. I wanted to but didn't want to. He put his arm on my shoulder and my immediate reaction was *yes* and *no*. I wanted him near but not too near.

For the next two weeks, whenever he'd come into the room, I felt extremely shy and tense till he had touched me, such as an arm around my shoulder or waist. Then I'd be OK. I fell in love with him at the emotional age of 15. The feeling went deep—very, very deep. It went as deep as the negative thing that had come out of me.

At age 17, cigarette smoke started to bother me. It got to the point where I had to drop a couple of clients (I was a self-employed housekeeper) because they were such heavy smokers. I had to make my apartment less susceptible to the smoke-filled hallway.

I remembered a trip that my grandma (Mom's mom) and I had taken while I was living with her during my high school years. We visited many of her relatives in Canada, and most of them were chain smokers. It was the first time I had come in close contact with smokers. At one place I almost passed out, but getting into the fresh air helped. I seemed to be having the same physical reaction the second time around.

Between the emotional ages of 12 and 18, I noticed I was having feelings I had trouble identifying. I felt more grown-up, as if I was maturing, leaving behind childish things. My emotions became more stable. I concluded I had been stuck emotionally between the ages of 8 and 12 right into adulthood. I was amazed at how I had been able to function on that level all those years.

I became disinterested in many things. I got tired of writing in my journal. I didn't feel like going to church any more. I didn't feel like doing much of anything. As a result, I now have very little written down about that time period.

One morning I woke up saying, "I do *not* want to go to work." I was experiencing being 22 years old for the second time, and I had taken only one whole week off since my change. If one year of emotional time was equal to one week of real time, it meant I had been working for twenty years over the last twenty-two weeks! No wonder I was exhausted.

CHAPTER 22

RELIVING AGES 23YRS TO 32YRS

A few days later, a new clergyman was called in the church ward. I didn't want to try to reacquaint a new one with my situation, so I quit going to church. During the rest of that week, I had a tension headache, which was very unusual for me. The emotional age I was experiencing corresponded with the age I had been when I went on my mission which was 21. The change in the clergy also paralleled the loss of the church president, who died three weeks after I left for my mission.

At the emotional age of 23, I went to CR's place and found out what he really thought of me. First, he said he liked me but didn't love me. He later changed that to he was "not in love" with me. Second, he pointed out that I was not very feminine, though more so than I had been before.

He said the reason I didn't seem feminine was "probably because you're overweight".

That comment blew me away. "Does my weight bother you?"

"To a certain degree."

"How much?"

He equated femininity with slimness. I went absolutely numb. I felt I was wandering around in a daze. I left crying.

The next day was a disaster. I slipped and fell on some ice on my way to work and hurt my hip. I broke my glasses as soon as I got to work. I started getting sick to my stomach around eleven o'clock that morning. I was crying and out of control. I went home and found out I'd lost my apartment keys, so I had to go over to my roommate's workplace and borrow hers.

My first crush came at 13 years old, my first love at 15, and my first heartbreak at 23.

As I grew mentally older, I felt myself maturing. I felt more responsible for my actions. My attention span increased. I started keeping all I was going through to myself and not telling the whole world. I was having feelings I had never felt before, as if I was really becoming an adult. I was more stable in my emotions, didn't take things as personally, and could see other people's stories. I redecorated my apartment in a more grown-up style. The more grown-up I became, the cleaner and less cluttered my environment became. I wanted everything to be new to suit the new me. I bought more feminine items: frills, lace, softly sexy clothes, and realistic art—though I still loved my teddy bears!

I decided to go home for Christmas and got very excited every time I thought of it. After all, it would be my first Christmas home in twenty-seven emotional years. I was just like a little kid—I couldn't wait to see what I got.

While at home, I attended the church supper and Christmas program. One lady commented, "Something's different about her. She's changed." Someone had noticed!

I managed to visit six people in nine days. It was very exhausting but a lot of fun. I was seeing these people for the first time and discovering how wonderful they really were. I especially enjoyed my visits with one sister and my brother. I had given them copies of Dad's letter. I now heard their feelings and thoughts. It was exciting to find out how we were all going through great changes in our lives, especially on the emotional level.

One church fellow I talked to had been to California for primal therapy counselling. He identified with what I had gone through. He likened our hang-ups to a Scripture passage: "I the Lord thy God am a jealous God, visiting the iniquity of the fathers upon the children unto the third and fourth generation of them that hate me" (Deut. 5:9 KJV). Our parents were first-generation members. They tried to live their faith perfectly all at once and became frustrated when they faltered. We children were the ones who suffered because of it. We could prevent much of the same thing from happening to our own children, thereby helping future generations.

This fellow also made the comment that he thought the reason for my church inactivity was because, to me, Dad meant religion. Since I had thrown Dad out of my life, religion went too.

I found myself still doing things I didn't want to do and hating myself for not saying no. I was asked to offer a prayer on a meal. I didn't want to but went ahead, as there was company in the room. I hated myself for doing it but decided I wasn't going to let it eat away at me and ruin my time at home. As soon as I made the decision, I felt better.

CHAPTER 23

1985

Around the third week in January, I seemed to catch up with myself. My emotional age felt like it matched my chronological age. I began living my "real" life. At the end of a day, I felt I had lived only one day and not a couple of months. I had more energy, and my life seemed to have slowed down. I began to enjoy the present and knew it wouldn't be gone in a fleeting moment.

After being a child for the second time, I had a great deal of self-confidence. I could do *anything*. Before my roommate left, she commented how hard she thought it would be for me to move out of that apartment. After all, it was where I had grown up!

On 10 March 1985, I decided to start writing this book. That day I reread my personal history and relived my life as a total female. I had thoroughly enjoyed it up until the move to the States. My childhood experiences were an absolute delight to live over again, and I appreciated the way I had written them.

My style changed as my inner conflict grew. Though I didn't feel much conflict reading it again, it was interesting to see how the inner conflict had affected my writing. What struck me were all the insights I had into what my real problem was, yet I still couldn't see it at the time. But then, I had never read my history all the way through since I had first written it. Perhaps I would have come up with the same answers.

It was difficult to read about my spiritual experiences in my prior life, as I was no longer interested in organized religion.

When rereading my comments about the ballet performance, I relived it as if for the first time. I couldn't shake the feeling I was having. I cried and cried. I couldn't read any further. I had to leave it for a week. Coming back to it, I still had the same reaction. I couldn't believe one so young could have so much pain and sadness inside her. I still get emotional thinking about it.

I read what I used to think about CR. I realized he was still the same, and I could no longer push away my doubts and fears. My biggest problem was trying to persuade myself that love was all that mattered. Even if I didn't like him, I knew I loved him. Why wasn't that enough?

I finally decided that love wasn't all that mattered. We broke up, or so I thought. I went back to him about a week later as a friend. Two very different feelings came over me, ones I had never felt before: I didn't *want* to be married, and marriage was no longer the only goal in my life.

I seemed to be living my life on a different level than before. I was no longer actively seeking religious truth. Previously, I had lived my life according to how guilty I felt. I now felt no guilt.

I now believe that a person should develop all aspects of their life as much as possible, these aspects being emotional, physical, mental, and spiritual states, with the spiritual enhancing all others. At this point I am not interested in the religious aspect, as in organized religion.

I went home in the summer of 1985, and for the first time I was able to have fun with Dad, laughing and joking around with him, feeling much more relaxed. I visited with Grandma (Mom's mom, who moved to Canada to be closer to family) and thoroughly enjoyed my visit. I used to avoid her as I could only see her as an extremely negative person, always complaining about something or someone. During this visit, I saw her as a person who did the best she could and was actually a neat gal.

These experiences gave me authority to speak for myself, but no one else. Everyone has their own story.

What was the new me like? I didn't masturbate any more, as it seemed to be a totally self-defeating behaviour. I didn't bake in new situations. I felt I had more control over my life. It became very important to me to find out, if I were ever to become pregnant, what the sex of my baby was before it was born, so I could start relating to it before birth. This was because I felt my experience had started even before I was born.

My intuitive feelings, if followed, always turned out to be right or true. I liked sports as much now as I did before. My periods became regular for the first time in my life: twenty-eight days on the nose. Previously, I had never known when they were due. They were always very erratic, some being forty-two days apart, others thirty, and so forth.

I was still the same industrious, dependable person as before, just totally female instead of part male, part female. The constant anger, unhappiness, and severe mood swings were all in the past.

I had had a fear of finding out that I was smart. I no longer had that fear. I knew I was smart.

My most recent roommate had gone through a similar experience. Both of us became like the families we had grown up in. Seeing the similarities between us and our families helped me to see that parents had a very important role to play in the lives of their children.

A song taken from the movie *Into the Woods* sums up my feelings regarding how parents can relate to their children:

Children Will Listen

By Stephen Sondheim

… Careful the things you say
Children will listen
Careful the things you do

Jennifer Gross

Children will see and learn
… Children will look to you for which way to turn
To learn what to be
Careful before you say "Listen to me"
Children will listen …

CHAPTER 24

AFTERMATH

Once I finished compiling the previous chapters, I found I did not want to write down another word—*ever*! I had kept journals for years, filling page after page with thoughts, feelings, and events, but once I finished this project, I couldn't write any more. It was if I had nothing more to say. Answers had been found. Questions quit coming.

Therefore, I didn't write again in any meaningful way until 2015. Christmas letters home are the only evidence of my life in the intervening years, and even those were very hard to do, as I just did not *want* to write. In fact, I didn't even want to read about my life, because what I had written for all those years was so negative. I went through all of my journals when writing my book. I decided I didn't want all that negativity around, so I burned all but one of them. What I write now is only from memory, and as the years go by, those memories are fading from overuse.

Because CR was basically a good guy, I eventually accepted a marriage proposal from him. Unfortunately, many things were not discussed during the courtship. Two weeks before the wedding, in August 1986, he told me something about himself that led me to tears. Instead of calling it off, I decided I would handle it later by trying to change him. Oops.

Besides this one issue, I discovered that assumptions are almost always wrong. Because CR had been raised in the same church, I *assumed* he thought the same way I did about many things. Having to wait a year to have kids was a major disappointment. Then I found I wasn't getting pregnant. I was tested for a whole year and found out I was normal. CR was tested and we found out it was his problem, not mine. We looked into adopting a Native American baby, but I didn't like the idea of an open adoption. I wanted complete control, even though I intended to encourage the child to learn of its heritage. I was thirteenth-generation Mohawk myself and had always been fascinated by the Native people's stories.

Why are you always behind a closed door? You don't show any feelings. I had these thoughts about CR. I dared not say them, remembering how Dad had always jumped down our throats for voicing our opinions or questions. CR did eventually say he felt smothered. He was very happy being an extreme loner. He had only two friends, a red flag that I didn't comprehend before our marriage.

I'm going to change his attitude, I thought. I complimented him constantly, left little notes in his lunches, and tried to be positive when discussing problems. Meals were ready when he came home, as my work schedule allowed me the time to cook.

After a year of knocking myself out to make sure he was happy and satisfied, I had nothing left to give. I felt completely drained. Nothing had changed. He was no more attentive to me than previously. He set up dates with fellow workers to play pool once a week. I didn't get the same consideration.

He wanted me to be more spontaneous, but I couldn't get past my need to control every situation. I was a planner, and hence a control freak who had to control not only my own situation but everyone else's.

We did go on some outings. We saw *Phantom of the Opera*, which I could have gone to once a week for a long time. The message and music really spoke to me. We went to a concert by a classical guitarist, as CR was interested in classical guitar. We had season's tickets for the city's pro football team. But most of these events were not conducive to intimacy.

Sex was OK. I battled the idea that before marriage, it was wrong and sinful, and then "I do" and it was OK? Having no transition period was confusing.

CR did support me when Dad passed away suddenly of a stroke in 1994. When I got the call, I was initially angry and upset. I was angry because I hadn't convinced Dad to relate to me as the "real" me, and upset that now he never would in this lifetime. It was all about me.

I began to feel that CR was emotionally immature. CR and I approached problems from totally opposite sides, him intellectually and me emotionally, though it fascinated me that we almost always came to the same conclusions.

He especially liked the ideas in some books I had read, a trilogy called *Conversations with God: An Uncommon Dialogue* by Neale Donald Walsch. According to Walsch, there is an opposition to all things. The opposition is not necessarily evil; it just is. I decided to live my life around this concept. I immediately felt free and unencumbered with guilt and shame for my thoughts and ideas. I felt my thinking expand as I could base my choices on the criteria. It was wonderful.

Synchronicity became a more dominant factor in my life as I started to notice coincidences. I have since concluded that there are no coincidences in life. All is part of a fantastic master plan, choosing what kind of life I really wanted and finding out what the consequences of my actions were.

I found out how to excel at math. I wanted to go to university, so I needed my grade 12 subjects, of which I only had English. *I'm so stupid* was a constant refrain in my head until I took the provincial Math 30 exam in 1987. In class I was failing and didn't know how I was going to pass. Then CR stepped in, he who knew *everything* about math (or so it seemed—he was a computer geek). He showed me a different way of approaching the subject, and I realized how I could do it. I would just memorize everything! And I did. That year the provincial exam was harder than it had been, because students and teachers had complained about it being far too easy the previous year. I had two weeks to pull it off. Final grade: 74 per cent!

Even though CR and I were both inactive except for church dances and social activities, church members still visited us monthly as per their duties. Shortly after we married, I was shocked when all the visitors' comments and questions were directed at CR as though I didn't exist. My opinions, of which I had many, weren't important. I hadn't realized how deeply engrained the concept of "head of the household" was in the church.

My work kept me busy, at least physically. I loved my clients, but the more I cleaned huge homes, the more I wanted a smallish house of my own.

I was hungry for a house. I had lived in apartments from the time I arrived in the city. Ten years later, now that we were married, I wanted a home. CR thought differently. He was interested in buying a duplex, then a four-plex, and gradually moving up to perhaps a sixteen-suite apartment building. It was his idea of retirement. It was a good idea, except I wasn't interested. I wanted a real home, garden, dog, and kids.

We did start out with a duplex that had one title, which we split. We built a rental suite in the basement of our side and eventually sold both halves. Since CR was a jack of all trades and master of most of them, he did all the work, from plumbing to electrical to installing appliances, flooring, and cupboards. Since we were on a limited budget, we scoured auctions and made some terrific deals. I discovered I liked renovating and fixing up things, except for hanging drywall and mudding.

Our first effort was not too bad. Next time, though, we decided to have a plan in place before trying it. When we finally moved into a house in 1991, we did a much more effective job of producing a very nice suite—though CR found out he needed to measure *everything*. He commissioned a company to cut legal-size holes for windows out of the basement concrete and gave them the measurements. He then made the frames. Alas, the frames didn't fit the windows. Mistakes are so enlightening.

Ah, peace and safe haven. Everything is going to be fine, I thought when I entered our first home. Then, *Maybe divorce? But how can I afford it?*

Instead, I said to CR, "We now have a house and a fenced yard. How about a dog?"

CHAPTER 25

ANIMALS

A few months later, one of my cleaning clients decided the dog they had obtained from the pound just wasn't working out. He was part German shepherd and part Scotch collie, and less than a year old. Sam became a member of our household in October 1992. Once I discovered his love of off-leash parks, some of which covered many acres, I committed to taking him every day. I didn't miss a day in two years.

Sam was a dog who was definitely more human than dog. When talking to him, you could see the wheels turning as he thought things through. We discovered we had to be careful what we said around him. He was eleven months old when we got him, and I wondered if he would ever be a watchdog. He looked mostly shepherd. Why wasn't he barking? He just seemed to be super happy when people came over.

I decided he had a lot of husky in him, as he'd play the hardest with any husky he met at the park. But he played with everyone, including those who didn't really want to at first. He had the happy-go-lucky attitude and bounce of a husky.

One day he did start barking—but at the back door, not the front. "I guess it's time to meet the neighbours," I said. He was about eighteen months old by then. Because he had a doggy door, he was already in the backyard by the time I got there. But he was barking at the alley end of the fence, not toward the neighbour's house. I saw someone running across the street. I later learned that the neighbours weren't home and that someone had tried to break in. The next day, Sam was at our feet when I told CR about the incident, and from that day forward, Sam barked at everything and everyone. It was uncanny.

One night I talked to CR about a client agreeing to let me bring Sam to work, so I could take him for a run in the off-leash area that was just outside their back door. The next morning, Sam was waiting at the front door when it was time for me to go to work, something he had *never* done before.

As many first-time dog owners notice, I felt Sam was lonely and could use a companion. So when I found a stray in the off-leash park, I took him in. This was in 1994. I found the owner eventually, but he was ready to give the dog up. Frisky was 7 or 8 years old, part Labrador and part malamute, whose siblings weighed eighty pounds plus. Being the runt, Frisky weighed only thirty-five pounds.

My education regarding pack behaviour had just begun. Frisky fought Sam for attention. Sam refused to stand up for himself. I learned the younger dog usually acquiesced to the older. I even attended a three day conference held outside of the city that was put on by behaviourists and veterinarians from *the* vet college in Ontario. Even though it was primarily for professionals such as dog trainers, vets and behaviourists, it was open to the public. I tried their recommendations and had instant success for a time. But I noticed that, if I spent five minutes petting Sam, Frisky felt he had a right to fight Sam. Because Sam had been there first, I felt it was unfair. Besides, Sam sulked a lot when Frisky was around.

Frisky also didn't seem to understand what play was all about at the off-leash parks. He would crowd me and try to hide behind me. If I put him on the leash, he calmed down immediately, which was the opposite of the usual reaction. Because he had often been tied up at his former home, not allowed to explore as a dog should, I tried to let him be a dog as much as possible. I let him run off-leash and supported him in new experiences. But he wasn't getting it. There was a gap in his ability to understand, as if there were a fog over his mind. After seven months, I tired of the constant fighting between him and Sam. So I found Frisky a good home with a client whose children fell in love with him. The feelings were mutual.

A homeopath near the city offered me a part-time job as an office assistant. In addition to homeopathy, herbs, nutritional supplements, and acupuncture were offered as healing remedies. I was fascinated by what could be done with natural products and a willingness to heal. It was a nice change from cleaning homes.

CR supported me when I wanted to do different things that many people considered weird:

homeopathy, the Tellington-TTouch method of healing, telepathic animal communication, and reiki. He always did like new ideas.

A few months later, I saw a poster in the off-leash area describing a holistic technique for dealing with problem dogs. I took Frisky to the three-day workshop as Sam didn't have any major problems. Tellington-TTouch is a way of moving skin that creates a healing effect at the cellular level—or at least that was the claim. After a minute and a half of being worked on, Frisky turned and looked at me. The fog had disappeared.

Two days later, I took Frisky and Sam to the off-leash park and Frisky *ran* with the big boys. He was playing his heart out. I was almost in shock. I had tried for seven months without success, and all it took was ninety seconds of being handled in a certain way for him to change his attitude. It was incredible. I thought, *Perhaps this is what I'm going to do for the rest of my life.*

A month or two later, I attended a three-day workshop dealing with problem horses and saw some amazing results. I was then handed some cassette tapes and was exposed to an intriguing idea. A gal in the States claimed she could communicate with animals by having conversations with them, similar to the way we humans communicate with each other. She said she did it in her mind via telepathy. *Whoa. Wait a minute*, I thought. *This is really weird.* But if it were true, what better way to find out what was going on with the animals than to ask them?

I immediately set up an appointment with a communicator to chat with one of our pet zebra finches, Miz, and with Sam. Miz was asked if she could let us know when she wanted out of her cage. She was not well and could not have any more babies. Because the males only wanted sex (or so it seemed), we were fearful of her inability to fend them off. She did seem to want to get out of her cage to socialize every once in a while.

The communication took place after nine o'clock in the evening, well after Miz had retired to her nest for the night. Once she entered the nest, the cage would have had to be turned upside down and shaken to dislodge her. The communicator, who was still in the States while I was in my hometown, said, "This is the sign when she wants out: she will run around on the bottom of the cage, look up, and start calling." I sat stunned. As the communicator was talking, Miz had hopped out of the nest and was running around on the bottom of the cage, looking up, and calling!

Sam was asked why he was so terrified of hot-air balloons. Our city was the hot-air balloon capital of Canada, and we saw them almost daily. The communicator didn't get a specific reason, but Sam acted differently the next day when we went to the park. It was as if he were saying, "Now that I know you know how much this bothers me, I can handle it better."

I thought, *I've got to learn how to do this.*

While preparing my suitcase for a trip to the States, Sam came in, nosing around to see if he was going too. "I'm going to the workshop to learn how to communicate with you," I told him. He immediately walked out of the room and didn't bother me again. On the plane, I sat beside an empty seat. Soon it was filled with the impression that Sam was sitting in it.

Never having been exposed to intuitive energy work, I was fascinated and a bit nervous. The first afternoon was spent working with other participants of the human persuasion, sending each other colours, scenes, and feelings via telepathy. The second afternoon was spent attempting to connect with the animals, including the teacher's chickens and bunnies. "Connect with your animal in a way that is comfortable for you," she said.

I invited Sam to come into my mind. He came in and sat in front of me.

"Send them a message."

I sent a yellow light full of love from my heart to his heart.

"Imagine them sending a message back to you."

I saw the yellow light travel from his heart to his head, back to my head, and down to my heart. When it reached my heart, I felt blown open, physically, mentally, emotionally, and spiritually. *I had done it!*

While I was marvelling at the overwhelming sensation of undeniable *knowing*, Frisky walked into my mind, followed by every animal I had ever known, most of them from the farm. I looked for Sam and found him in a corner of our backyard, grinning from ear to ear. Yes, I could now communicate with all of them on a much different level.

I was reborn and ready for a new name. "Jennifer" conjured up images of a pretty little blond girl laughing and running joyously through ripened wheat fields. When the notary public stamped the official papers with his seal, the overwhelming feeling was: *Yes, this is so right!* I felt liberated from the old me, from "Miriam".

I became an official telepathic animal communicator in October 1996. Aside from my wonder at the many animal stories I've heard, it has given me great satisfaction to teach the skill to others. I'm still blown away when people start connecting with animals they have never met and receiving very accurate information.

I loved the media attention I received. I was interviewed by local and national radio stations and a local TV station. I enjoyed contributing to changing people's awareness concerning the world's animals. I finally felt validated as a good, helpful person.

CHAPTER 26

CHANGE OF SCENERY

I enrolled in an interior decorating course as a back-up to my animal business and found that I loved doing floor plans, arranging furniture, and working with colours.

CR and I couldn't seem to make any headway in our relationship, even though we tried counselling. We acted on one suggestion: that we live apart for a while and see how we felt. It was a breath of fresh air for both of us. We decided to make it permanent.

I moved to my home province in July 2002 with my dog Sam. I moved back because I missed water and trees, two of the province's very dominant features. Because I had been a housekeeper for many years and had cleaned some large homes, I wanted a small house on an acreage.

I started out living with my mom in town, as I didn't know where I wanted to live other than *not* in that particular town. It seemed to have a dark, controlling cloud over it so far as alternative thinking attitudes were concerned. Mom wanted her house fixed up, and I lived there while I did the work. It took me seven months, working six days a week.

Since she wouldn't let me work Sundays, I used those days to go house hunting. After a few months, I awoke one day with the thought, *Since you told everyone you were moving back to Manitoba because of trees and water, check out this town.* I found a mobile home sitting on a third of an acre with twenty-five trees, a garage, a fenced yard, all gardening and lawn equipment, and even a double sink in the kitchen—absolutely *everything* I had been looking for. And the 12 square mile lake is only 15 minutes away.

I moved in on 2 November 2002, and it has been my safe haven ever since.

It took me at least seven months to decompress from the stresses of loss: moving from a place I'd lived for twenty-five years and a divorce after sixteen years of marriage and twenty-four years of relationship. I had no work, no support group, no animal communication clients, and no home of my own. Add in menopause—I literally thought I was going crazy because my memory decided to take an extended vacation during the seven-month renovation project.

Crawling out of a hole, I reassessed my life.

I tried to work as an animal communicator but found it tough slogging. A bigger city that was much more open to alternative thinking became my work area. I travelled six hours round trip to teach workshops and do consultations. I did many more consults from the comfort of my own home, over the phone.

On occasional trips to the west, I heard that CR had found a new gal and was teaching her how to dance. They had a common interest in rocketry and remote-controlled airplanes. She was also extremely thin, just his type.

At the suggestion of one of my sisters, I joined an organization geared to helping people learn how to give more effective presentations and lectures. I discovered I loved giving speeches and was relatively good at it, even winning a speech contest. Writing speeches resurrected my interest in perhaps editing this book and preparing it for publication. In 2008, I let someone other than family read it. Though they thought it was worthy of publication, I still did not have the heart to do anything with it.

Because my animal work was almost nil, I became a receptionist at a seniors home in my mom's town in 2008. About the same time, Mom was looking for someone to live with her. I made the decision to move in with her and immediately resented it. Family comes first, right? It seemed an OK fit at first, as I was having problems with frozen pipes at my place. I started living a few days with Mom and a few days at my place. It was nearly impossible to run a side business when I was not at home and needed something that would take an hour and a half to retrieve. It seemed to be a constant war of trying to remember everything I would need for a few days at a time. It was very frustrating to believe I had thought of everything, only to find out I hadn't. I finally let go of the animal business and only went home on my days off to check on the house and cats.

I felt trapped once again.

CHAPTER 27

STRESS

My work at the senior's home included the responsibility of looking after people whose health problems I was not allowed to know because of privacy legislation. This was very stressful. I never knew what kind of a situation I would be walking into. I couldn't control much of anything. Meanwhile, the manager seemed to love being in the thick of things and micromanaging.

I started on the 12 a.m. to 8 a.m. shift, which gave me a lot of time to work on my speeches but left me short of sleep. After a year plus, I went to the 4 p.m. to 12 a.m. shift, which was better sleep-wise. But because of the rotation for working weekends, it left me with no time for anything extra, like classes, outings, and so forth. I couldn't even go to my beloved speech meetings. I felt cut off from everything except work, plus I was living in someone else's home.

The stress escalated.

Every six months, I vowed I was going to quit work. I didn't appreciate the playing of favourites among the staff, the egos involved, or the catering to the ridiculous whims of a head office fifteen hundred miles away. My only problems were that it was a steady pay cheque, and many of the residents became lifelong friends.

Two years later, in 2010, my left leg weakened inexplicably. Stroke and MS were ruled out. I was left severely off balance, and when I walked the halls at work, I would almost crash into them. I could no longer run down the halls or climb stairs quickly during an emergency. I was afraid I'd be fired if anyone found out how bad I was. I managed somehow.

A change of directors didn't help my stress level. The new one did absolutely nothing, and the problems piled up. Another director change occurred, and we all had high hopes. These were justified for the first couple of months.

Around this time, in 2014, I had new well pipes put in my yard. Then Mom decided she wanted to move to an apartment to get away from the responsibilities of having to rake her lawn and sweep snow off the sidewalk at age 92.

We had about seven months to get the house ready, repairs that were mostly cosmetic but nonetheless time-consuming, for a spring sale. I set up a project schedule and was two months into it when I realized I had to do my taxes right in the middle of everything! I was at home when I realized this, so I went into my office to get receipts. I immediately noticed the carpet was wet under my desk. Moisture was halfway up some boxes sitting on the floor. I called the plumber and started hauling out everything: boxes, a file cabinet, bookshelves, a six-foot-square desk, and all the computer stuff.

Then the plumber couldn't find the leak! It wasn't anywhere near where the new pipes had come into the house. He even cut holes in the floor to see the condition of the sewer pipes. The insulation was dry. He had been *sloshing* in water just a day before. He climbed the roof but saw no problem there either—no moisture running down the walls or in any other room. There was no leakage in the bathroom right next to the office. *Nothing!*

My living room, kitchen, and hallway were now filled with office stuff. I knew I would have to get new flooring at some point, but I felt I couldn't deal with it right then. Maybe after Mom's house was done.

By February 2015, I was ahead on her project schedule and finally decided to look for flooring for my house. I found what I wanted, bought it on the spot, and brought it home, though I knew it would be months before it would be installed.

Always on the lookout for new DVDs, on this same shopping expedition I came across *Glee*. I had vaguely heard about it over the years, something about teens and music. I had dismissed it as not having the kind of music I was interested in, namely anything before the 1980s. So what was all the fuss about? I didn't find time to watch them.

In April, Mom got word she had an apartment for May. I got busy boxing up stuff for the move and preparing for a garage sale.

My work situation seemed to be easing for a while, but then down came the hammer and it was micro-micro-micromanaging time again. Because

I had the evening shift and I was extremely organized, I always got everything done—when *I* could do it. The new boss started telling me when to do what. That approach didn't fly with me. The day I was accused of something I didn't do, I gave notice.

Thank goodness, Mom supported me. She had been my sounding board for the past two years when things got really bad. She could always see at least two sides to any argument and could discuss things with calmness and clarity, qualities I greatly admire.

My last day at work ended on 30 April at midnight. Less than eight hours later, I was moving Mom into her apartment. Because I wanted to have the place all set before she showed up, I spent at least four hours unpacking and arranging. It was exhausting.

I decided to have a garage sale two weeks later so the house would be relatively empty when it sold. The sale took me four days to organize. I wanted to have the house act as the "garage", so I brought all the lightweight items (furniture, clothes, bedding) up from the basement and spread them throughout the house. Kitchen stuff was laid out on the kitchen counters, living room stuff was in the living room, yard and garden tools were in the shed, and so forth. I did most of the work as everyone else worked during the day, and what little energy I could muster was always highest during the day. I was still living there anyway, so at least I wasn't adding driving time.

I was tired, and my leg protested most of the time. When it got tired, my toes curled and threw me off balance even more than usual. I would end up stumbling over the slightest height difference on the floor or ground.

The sale was a success, though there were only about two minutes out of the whole day when there wasn't someone going through the house. I went to my home for the weekend, having decided that on Monday I would pack up the remainder of the sale and take it to a charity.

I had asked some churchwomen to come by and help me clean for future open houses. On Monday, after packing up everything and dropping off seven boxes at the charity, I walked into the house with the intention of gathering the few remaining pieces of furniture into one room to make cleaning easier. The thought hit: *Sit down or you are going to lose it mentally—you will become a blubbering idiot.*

I sat down. I couldn't focus on what to do or think of next, so I stayed sitting and just watched as the women arrived and cleaned the house.

Mom's house didn't sell right away. I drove into town once a week to check on Mom, take her shopping, and stay overnight at the house just to keep an eye on it. I had left a bed, as well as some canned soup, a bowl, a pot, and a spoon for meals. The fridge and stove were still there, as was a TV, a DVD player, and a rocker-recliner that I had moved in five years previously.

Meantime, I still had to deal with the mess in my own home. All my office stuff was still in the living room, hallway, and kitchen. I found someone who could lay new flooring on the last Monday of May.

The following Monday, 1 June 2015, I received a call from out west. One of my best friends, the intellectual one who had given me Eda LaShan's book, had passed away. The funeral might be on

Saturday. I started making a list of what to take on my car trip.

Tuesday, 2 June 2015, I moved all my stuff to my home, with the exception of my rocker-recliner. My new office floor had just been installed and looked lovely. Later that evening, I found out the funeral was being held Thursday morning, not Saturday. I had to leave the next day to make it in time. While frantically throwing things in a suitcase, I realized I had no reason to hurry back—I didn't have a job, Mom's house was ready, and Mom was adjusting to her new apartment. Everything had fallen into place for me to take off with no return date.

Speeding down the highway, the tension and stress sloughed off me like dead skin. I felt lighter and lighter until I was practically floating down the road. I thought, *I'm free.*

I reconnected with people I hadn't seen in many years, and it was grand. Two weeks later, I was in my own home again. I was excited about living in my own place and getting back on track with my animal business.

CHAPTER 28

FORMALDEHYDE & "GLEE"

I returned home on Monday evening, 15 June 2015, and was in the hospital on Thursday afternoon, 18 June, suffering from formaldehyde poisoning. I had reacted to the formaldehyde in my new flooring. My neck and face swelled up red as a beet, with one eye almost closing. I was advised not to return to my home when I left the hospital the next day. A friend retrieved some clothes for me, and I drove straight to my mom's still-unsold house.

I thought, *Why can't I live in my house? Why am I so devoid of feelings again? I have so much work to do: yard work, promoting my animal business, and so on and so on and* so on.

All I had at Mom's house were some cans of soup (though I had forgotten a can opener!), a TV, a VHS player and a DVD player—and six seasons of *Glee*.

I started watching *Glee* and instantly sympathized with Kurt, the gay kid, and his painful struggles with life. I realized how much similar pain I was carrying around with me. I knew my mental, emotional, and physical selves were on the verge of total collapse, and if I didn't change, I would die.

The music resonated deeply in my soul. I've always been more interested in what story the music is telling than in the mere singing of a song. Coming from a musical family, I could appreciate the quality of voices, harmonies, and sentiments expressed.

The following is part of a letter I wrote on 11 August 2015, to a *Glee* cast member less than two months after starting to watch *Glee*:

> I now realize the almost empty house [*Mom's house*] was a metaphor for my empty soul. I had been under so much stress from not allowing myself to be me for at LEAST the past six years, that I literally felt nothing, no positive vibes, no negative ones, absolutely barren of all feelings. I was as empty as the house.
>
> Since I had quit work in May I had a lot of time with no energy so I could only sit. I

couldn't focus on very much at one time, so why not watch Glee. I watched and watched and watched, sometimes for twenty four hours straight.

Kurt drew me into the show but it was the music that started the healing process. After a solid 2 weeks of just Glee – no newspapers, no radio, almost no outside contact, I finally opened my mouth to sing along with the music. The flood gates opened and along with the tears, realizations poured out:

1. I have a passion for music: perhaps it's why I bought a little keyboard when I moved into my house back in 2002. I don't play it, but I have to have a musical instrument in my home.

2. I have a passion for dance. If I really work at it my arthritic knee and weak left leg will allow me to recapture some ballroom steps.

Wonderful.

Little bits of joy started bubbling up in my soul.

Another week or two passed (weak memory) and I found myself starting to laugh at the puns, comedic timing of facial expressions, the obnoxious comments of

Sue Sylvester, Tina's backward episode, the Bruce arm, and so forth. Hilarious.

[*Along with my emotions*] My life's baggage then started showing up, claiming top spot on my recovery list. After the 4th run through all six seasons, Korofsky's suicide attempt hit me like a ton of bricks. I finally reacted as memories of my own "incident" surfaced. That episode started a chain reaction in me finally being able to react emotionally to each episode as I saw it. I was starting to live in the now. I went through all six seasons again feeling like it was for the very first time. Wonderfully therapeutic.

The music also became much more powerful in drawing out those feelings. The songs most important to me became: "Being Alive" as I felt I was crowding me with love, "And I'm Still Here" and "I Am Changing". Because of the intimacy, my all time favorites are "A House is Not a Home", "One hand, One Heart" and the incomparable "Come What May".

Butterflies became prominent in my life again, all about transforming from one stage in life to another and participating in their Dance of Joy. "I am finally starting to feel ALIVE." [*Whenever I did dare to go home, butterflies surrounded me as a sat in my yard.*]

Simply put: "Glee" saved my life. Thank you.

Mom's house was pulled off the market, as I didn't know how long it would take to decontaminate my house. The floors of my house were washed twice a day for two weeks, and I ran fans 24/7. Once a week I would try to go back but would react within fifteen minutes. I would feel tingling in my right hand that I soon learned was an early stage of reaction. It wasn't enough to put me in the hospital though, thank goodness. In response, I would down some homeopathics, and within a half hour, the symptoms would subside. All I could do was wait it out.

While waiting, I continued to have insight after insight of what I had given up during the last six years and how my body had almost collapsed because of it.

More *Glee* insights: on Aug. 25, I noted how I cried when Sam's guitar was returned to him. I cried because of his and my love of music. I have always felt that there must be a musical instrument in the home, even if it isn't being used.

"Oh, there you are." That statement had always been my absolute favourite line in the whole series, and I didn't know why until I was at Mom's sink one day, washing dishes. "Oh, here I am. This is the real you. This person who loves music, dance, joy, life, and the fact that it's never too late to change!" What an affirmation.

My weak left leg was starting to feel better. I could walk up small inclines and not feel off balance.

Once, my brother came by Mom's house, and I mentioned how I had resented my decision to live with Mom and how it had festered in me. His reaction? "Make another choice." So simple, yet so far beyond my comprehension at the time.

I had a dream. It was very rare for me to remember my dreams. An intruder came into a living room, which was not the living room in my house or my mom's house. I woke myself up with a scream, something I had never been able to do regardless of how bad a nightmare I had been having. *I was starting to stick up for myself!*

I had quit painting pictures back in 2008 when I developed blood clots in my legs from sitting still for hours on end filling in paint-by-number kits. I painted a picture. *Creativity was coming to the fore!*

My voice was getting stronger. When I talked with a friend, she complained I was *loud*, which was not my usual speaking self unless I was complaining about something. *I was speaking my truth, not caring who heard it.*

My singing voice was improving. When I first started singing with *Glee*, my voice cracked all over the place, though I had been singing fine two months before. I started to harmonize with *Glee*, and one day I sang and stayed *on key.* Exciting!

I occasionally had access to a computer, and I looked up *Glee* and the actors and actresses who performed in it. One of the actors had written some books about fairy tales. I got a couple of them and laughed myself silly. Much of his third book was *Glee*-inspired.

I looked at all the magic that had happened in my life over the preceding couple of months and found myself starting to dream again. I even got a license plate that said IMGN IT. Imagine it.

During August and September, I had a couple of readings from a psychic. Some animals showed up. One was a beetle, which was all about resurrection and putting the past behind oneself. Another was a rooster, which was all about sexuality. I had been getting turned on lately, starting to come alive. A rabbit meant good fortune for up to four months after the reading. Maybe I would move back to my place? The rabbit also meant fertility, new life, sensitivity, and artistry.

The raccoon was fascinated by water, which increased sensitivity of hands and also heightened telepathic abilities. I had received many telepathic messages from animals when washing dishes. The raccoon mask had powerful mystical symbolism. It was a tool for transformation. It would help to change what I was to what I chose to be, giving me magic. And a hummingbird reminded me to find joy in what I was doing and sing it out. The hummingbird's ability to fly backwards meant to explore the past and draw from it the nectars of joy.

Every time I have come to a point in my life when I haven't known which way to turn, I've gotten a reading, and many animals have pointed the way. In 1996, I participated in an animal communicator workshop for those wanting to teach the instructor's basic course. The instructor told me that the animals would heal me. They still loved doing it.

With a song in my heart, "I've come home at last", I was finally able to move back home on 12 December 2015, almost exactly six months to the day I'd had to leave it. A day later, my industrial fan quit. It had been going 24/7 since June. I still felt a little uneasy health-wise, but I was not getting a full-blown reaction.

About a week later, Mom fell and sustained a compression fracture in her back. A couple of weeks later, I woke up one morning feeling perfectly safe. Why?

I was making meals for Mom, and they all had onions in them. I knew that onions were supposed to be good for taking flu out of the air, but I didn't realize they also got rid of formaldehyde. I started putting out onions whenever I used my brand-new washer and dryer and printer, as I could smell the formaldehyde pouring off them. I would feel safe again after a day or two. Thanks, Mom, for your broken back! Thank you, onions!

CHAPTER 29

ANOTHER JOURNEY

Shortly after I returned home, I realized that my summer experience was the perfect ending to the book I had written back in 1985.

When I started to come out of my self-imposed hibernation or emotional breakdown in mid-July, I found I could not stay focused on any one thing for very long. I could not plan for more than maybe two days ahead.

When the house sold in September for possession in December, Mom suggested we take a trip out west to see our health practitioner. I immediately wilted under the weight of that suggestion. Too much planning had to go into such a trip, and I couldn't wrap my head around it.

Every once in a while, I would think of a time when I might be ready to go back to work as an animal communicator, but I couldn't project when that might be. It was an odd experience, as I usually had my life organized at least six months in advance. I'd always known I was going to get my book ready for publication at some point in my life, but was never motivated to actually sit down and do it. Now it just seemed far too overwhelming, as did everything else in my life.

As the months of confinement went by, I found I was able to stay focused on an idea for longer periods of time. I was actually able to organize a work party to help put the office stuff back when I moved home in December. I was very proud of myself.

By February 2016, I was starting to think seriously about getting back in the swing of things regarding my business. I got new business cards printed up, booked space in two animal communication workshops I wanted to attend out west in April, and paid for a pet expo exhibit and lecture being held in May in Mom's town. Finishing those few tasks was a huge accomplishment. My back was sore from all the self-pats.

I was excited to attend the animal communication workshops. I had been teaching the first one ever since I started my business in 1996, but I hadn't been able to take it as a student, as there had been no one in the area who taught it.

As participants, we communicated with each other's animals, whom we'd never met. We didn't communicate with our own as we knew ours too well and couldn't trust the messages coming through. Almost all the animals I connected with, as well as all of mine whom others connected with, said the same thing: "Write the book!" I had told *no one* about the book!

When I got home, I went into full exhibit mode for the pet expo. Because my exhibit was so unique, I received very good coverage from two radio stations and the province's main newspaper. My lecture touched quite a few hearts and I was hopeful of seeing a full workshop in three weeks.

One person came. She did extremely well, even telling me the exact same message that one of my dogs had told a communicator out west in April. The two communicators had never met.

I held another workshop at the end of June, but no one signed up.

It was time to crack open the book.

The task still felt very overwhelming until I had the thought, *Read it through with no thought of editing it to see if it still says what you want it to.* I did and it did. Because I didn't react emotionally to the story, almost as if I hadn't really lived it, I felt I was ready to start pulling it apart.

But before I could, I had to do some research. I could no longer remember the scripture quotations Dad had used, so I had to reread the Bible and other church scriptures. I garnered about twenty pages' worth of quotations, written out in longhand.

I then reread book 1 of *Conversations with God.* I cried almost all the way through it. Much of it struck home, particularly the idea that we *choose* to create our lives. I had deliberately *chosen* to become a boy to please others. I hadn't thought of it in quite those terms before, so it hit me like a ton of bricks. I am a pleaser, and that had been the ultimate way to please—to become exactly what someone else wanted me to be.

Two other books had made an impact on my life, so I reread them also: *The Secret* by Rhonda Byrne and *One Day My Soul Just Opened Up* by Iyanla Vanzant. Two main themes in these books are gratitude and how like attracts like (synchronicity).

I finally realized why I was being pushed to finish this book. My story is all about gender identity. It seems there is a fascination right now about the topic, raging around the world or at least in the Americas. I believe *Glee* had something to do with it. The show gave those of a different gender preference a much-needed voice and a hope for a life that was not under constant scrutiny, judgement, and ill-will.

In all of my readings of the Bible and other scriptures, one has always risen up to be the most important for me: "Thou shalt not judge" (Matt. 7:1 KJV) If we all actively pursued this course of thinking and doing, tolerance and love would be much easier to implement.

I cannot condone what is happening in the transgender world right now though. I understand that some children, 4 to 5 years old, are having gender reassignment surgery. These are *children!* Just because a child may be leaning a bit toward one sex or the other in so-called sex-appropriate play behaviour, whatever *that* means, does not mean it is because they were born to be a different sex. I can understand loving and supporting differences, but please do not intentionally steer children toward a specific goal. When they are older—say, 9, 10, or 11—gender identity can be discussed in depth and decisions can be made by *everyone*, with the help of professionals. If I had had the procedure done and *then* found out I was female, where would I be? Some folks say being gay is a sin. If it is, I believe what the doctors are doing right now is a greater one.

I have just read an article in the 15 February 2014, issue of *MacLean's*, "Transgender kids: Have we gone too far?" I'm a behaviourist at heart. Wait and see. Provide opportunities for all points of view. Parents, teachers, general humanity: let's give them love and acceptance and see where it leads.

I have no quarrel with non-heterosexuals, although I didn't start out that way. I had agreed with what I had been taught while growing up: that homosexuality was a sin and I should not associate with "them". When I started conducting my animal communication workshops, I found many of those who attended were lesbians. I decided that gays and lesbians loved their animals just as much as the rest of us did, and I liked all whom I met.

I didn't know much about transgender people until I watched *Glee*. I had seen some guys in drag and thought they were weird. Now I just think we're all weird. So what? I still think the definition of marriage shouldn't have changed, as that's what it has always meant. Since the definition has changed, though, I've really no objections. I just can't believe that we all don't have the same rights to live life without judgement.

This movement has a long way to go. I am reminded of the women's movement of the 1960s and how long it took before banks allowed single women to borrow money for a home or a business. I would have had a more difficult time in the 1970s and 1980s if I had been seeking a mortgage to buy my little house then. Hang in there, folks, and keep fighting.

CHAPTER 30

LETTING GO

What were they thinking?

I felt disappointment, emotional devastation.

The church had put out the call for us members to do everything we could to stop California from approving gay marriage, essentially telling members that the families and children of homosexuals weren't loved by God. When all was said and done, according to some reports, over one hundred thousand people left the church even though church authorities later apologized.

My life's anchor was gone. I would find my God elsewhere.

Some *Glee* cast members were guests on *Inside the Actor's Studio*, and they were asked, "What would you like to hear God say when you meet him at the pearly gates?"

I cherish the response given by one who was gay: "Don't listen to them. You get to come in too." Priceless.

171

EPILOGUE

September 2019

What are my feelings and thoughts today?

I do like myself for trying to find answers and trusting that what I find will not devastate me but will be wonderfully enlightening.

I am still very short on people skills and feelings of self-worth. Because I have kept to myself and the church for so many years, I find my social skills wanting. I initiate conversations when I want something. I am just now realizing what it means to be a friend: enjoy each other's company, help out when asked, rejoice in their triumphs, and listen to their inner revelations, whether or not they do the same for me.

Love and fear cannot abide in the same space at the same time. Most of my life has been lived in fear. Fear of failure stops me from even trying and fear of success stops me from progressing. I have become a great spectator of life, terrified of actually putting myself out there to try living. Finishing this book has been difficult. Now it's going to be out in the world and what will people think? I keep relying on one thought "If it helps just one person to pause and think it's been worth it."

I have protected myself by being overweight. Food has become my refuge from fear.

I seem to have lost all curiosity, the ability to question. I always accepted the status quo. If I asked questions about another person's life, it felt like prying. I have a very curious sister, and she constantly asks questions about everything. It doesn't occur to me to ask questions. I wonder about things but don't ask for further knowledge.

When faced with a highly controversial subject, I convey my opinions with great passion, many times with anger born out of frustration at perceived ignorance or lack of common sense. I go right back to my upbringing and the way I used to react.

I find it quite difficult if not impossible, to make decisions as to what I want out of life. All my life I was willing to 'obey' how others thought I should live my life. Because work and chores always came first, play is almost a foreign concept. Now that I am semi-retired, I don't know where to put my energies. Guess it's time to take up a hobby.

I still struggle with my left brain versus right brain sides at least on the physical level. I understand that the left brain manifests itself physically on the right side of the body, female the left. My left side has: poorer eyesight, lost more teeth, had a lump removed, and sustains mild Bell's Palsy and a dropped foot.

I asked my mom what kind of kid I was. "Very helpful," she replied.

I asked my brother what he thought of me growing up. "A brother," he replied. That was my life in a nutshell – a helpful son who abandoned herself at birth. Time to see a therapist.

I have a picture of a cross-stitched wolf (my power animal) hanging in my living room. The message reads "Follow Your Heart with Gentleness". This reflects how I think of my parents. My dad was all about following his heart. Mom lives her life with gentleness. I am trying to do the same.

Between the two of them, my parents did a decent job. All their children turned out to be positive contributors to society.

To people everywhere, in your judgements of others, remember that we are all unique. Some self-defeating attitudes and behaviours are more visible than others. We all judge, but it's what we do with those judgements that tell us what kind of person we are. Judgement to me is just discernment of whether or not I want to emulate a certain quality.

We live in a world of opposites. As I see it, our only decision is what we do with the information we receive. I believe we are all given free choice. Given the choices we have, we can only do what we feel is right for us. That doesn't mean we have to ostracize others to live our lives more meaningfully. We can uplift anyone with a kind word, a gesture, and so forth. Let's be willing to at least hear each other's stories.

My soul always holds the truth about me. It reminds me of Who I Am and chooses Who I Wish to Be. I have a right to my joy. I will seek it and find it. My goal is to choose love in *all* situations.

Support and love are two of God's greatest gifts.

May we all be so blessed.

Printed in the United States
By Bookmasters